The Remnant

Micah Four: Six and Seven;
The Ancient Book.

*A Fiction
By*

Lori Hankins

xulon
PRESS

The Remnant
by Lori Hankins

Printed in the United States of America

Library of Congress Control Number: 2003092243
ISBN 1-591607-12-4

All scripture is taken from: The Holy Bible. New International Version, Ultra Thin Reference Edition. Broadman & Holman Publishers. Nashville, Tennessee. Copyright © 1984.

Xulon Press
www.XulonPress.com

Xulon Press books are available in bookstores everywhere, and on the Web at www.XulonPress.com.

The power of God rests in the weak and foolish things of the world, confounding the wisdom built upon mans' shallow intelligence.
Our God will not contend with men, and finding impossibility His best ally in the fallen race, once again the time is ripe for visitation.

Change is in the wind, the wind is of the Spirit....

Chapter One

S usan smiled as she stood looking at her reflection in the mirror. Turning from side to side, puckering her lips and brushing her light brown hair over her head in showgirl fashion, she thought about herself, and who she really was. She was just an average, run-of-the-mill type person. Medium height and weight, brown hair, hazel eyes. There was nothing romantic about her description anyway. She stopped and came close to the mirror, looking deep in her own eyes. Now maybe if she had blue eyes, or brown eyes, then there might be some love song that she could pretend was about her, but whoever heard of a love song about a girl with hazel eyes? She stood back and put her hands on her hips. Shaking her head back and forth, she let out a sigh. It wasn't that she was critical about herself; she was thankful that she didn't stand out in an unusual way and attract attention to some distinctive body part. No, she would rather be plain than noticeable. From what she had been able to discern about life, plain people lived ordinary lives, lives that didn't have horrible things happen, or at least that was what her young mind told her.

She was 23 years old, and quite independent. She had a couple of close friends, a job and an apartment of her own. Even her name was common, but she did have a secret hope of someday meeting that special man that would change everything, and of course his name would be exotic, like something out of the movies. 'Susan Jones' was definitely average to her, but on the other hand she knew that there was much more to a person than a name. She slowly backed away from the mirror and sat on the soft, floral bedspread. She gently fingered the rose pattern, following the gentle curves of the pedals, letting her thoughts wander about like a butterfly happily in search of sweet nectar on a lazy spring day.

What Susan didn't realize was that she was indeed quite different. She had spent many an hour contemplating the mysteries of the universe and of all creation. And that, not in an ordinary way, for she was known in the heavens as 'One who searches for true answers.' In fact, she was often the topic of heavenly conversations between angels who had been assigned to her, and those who vied for that coveted position. For in all the earth, there were very few such as her. She would never be content with all the pat answers that she had heard. Because to her, those 'pat' answers, as she called them, did not add up to what she was seeing and feeling about the life around her.

She was not a religious type person, mostly because she didn't see most religious people as ones who asked questions and sought answers for themselves. To her they seemed to be content with whatever their religion told them, and when questioned they didn't have any better answers about all of creation than the rest of the world. They did have an Ancient book that they often referred to, but again, to her most of them had little understanding of even the book that they said they were being guided by. Well, in her mind that was simply crazy.

Maybe some of the problem with her inability to accept religion was the fact that she had not been raised in the church like many people had. She supposed that if she were taught religious ways from childhood on, it would be more easy to accept. But her lot in life was not so simple. Her mother had abandoned her as a baby, and she did not know who her father was. Most of her youth had been spent in one foster home or another. She had not been fortunate enough to find a family who would keep her. Maybe her need to know about all the mysteries was somehow related to her need for roots. She did not know.

One thing that she did know was that there was more than empty space out there and it held the answers to all her questions. For some strange reason, Susan felt as though whatever was out there, it was waiting for her to come and find it. She had felt strangely protected by whatever 'it' was all her life. To her it had almost seemed as though there were some sort of invisible Dad out there watching over her. She knew that many kids who grew up as she did, were usually really messed up and insecure. But whatever had protected her, it had given her a confidence in herself that kept her from needing the drugs and promiscuity that her peers ran after.

She had never been able to share these secret thoughts with anyone though. She felt for sure that they would say she was making it all up, that it was 'her way of coping' or some 'alter-ego' thing that she had made up along the way. But in truth, she had been shown things that she knew she could never make up. These 'showings' had got her to thinking the most. It seemed that they had come when she had asked questions. One time, in her way of deep pondering, she had blurted out the question, "Is there really a purpose to all this?" Then something happened so fast that she caught her breath, and tried to keep the image of it foremost in her mind. It was as though the space in front of her had peeled away, and she was standing in outer space. There was a great light that somehow seemed to hold all truth and life in it. Then, just as suddenly, she was right back where she had been. She was left with a wonderful feeling that everything was okay out there. She had spent many an hour contemplating what she had experienced but was unable to define for herself what had really happened.

In the unseen realm Adaiah was sitting close by. He was the primary angel in Susan life, though he didn't think of her as Susan. 'Bilshan,' that was her true name. For she was a searcher, a seeker of truth. He had been with Bilshan from the first day of her life on the earth, and he loved her as much as an angel could love a human soul. He also knew about the call on her life, that from the womb she (along with a remnant of other searchers) had been chosen to find and follow the ancient path.

He looked to the day, one that was quickly approaching, when he would be able to speak with her and begin showing her the mysteries that had been locked up until the 'time of the end.' All of creation had been crying out for the revealing of this remnant who would bring in the ancient way of truth. The immortal angel, being able to see both the physical and the spiritual realms, was more than ready for creations 'cries' to be answered. The King of Glory Himself was preparing a great feast to usher in the new age to come.

Now is the time, thought Adaiah, *for the ancient way to be brought back. The great ingathering of souls is about to begin. How long we and the great cloud of witnesses have waited.* The angel sighed. *Bilshan, if you could see how they are gathered, waiting and watching for the unveiling that is about to begin. If you could only see these souls who have lived and died embracing the One from whom they have received eternal life, you would surely rejoice and long for the final day as I do.*

But they, the great cloud of witnesses, were few in number compared to that great and vast majority of lost souls who were yet to receive the truth. The earth itself had become so dark and full of demonic legions that were bringing about the fullness of the Antichrist spirit. Adaiah knew that his assignment with Bilshan was of major importance to the multitudes of lost people that her life would have an impact upon. There was much at stake during this time in history, for there was a culmination of evil that had been building up and being released since the very beginning of time.

The sins of the fathers had been visited upon the children of the earth to the degree that the evil was almost equal to the days of Noah, a flood of filth covered the same earth that a few thousand years ago was covered with cleansing water.

Even now, as he looked over at Bilshan, who was sitting close to him and looking out into space as if searching for him, he thought of how many times the enemy had tried to kill her. She was oblivious to this fact, since Adaiah had been able to call for his company of soldiers in time to avert many disasters. He almost laughed to himself as he thought of how Bilshan was thinking to herself that being ordinary meant that she was safe from disaster. The fact that she felt ordinary, was really the disguise that had been put upon her at the time of her birth to keep her safe until the appointed time. She was by far more than an ordinary person, for to be chosen for such a mission as she had been was indeed a great privilege.

Funny, he thought, *how these humans can only see with eyes of the flesh. They have no idea what they are looking at. They judge beauty by its external appearance, having no thought or understanding of how things really stood. The outer cloak of the flesh was only a garment, and though to the eyes some might have nicer garments than others, it really had nothing to do with what was inside of the person.*

Once, while Bilshan was a young child living with a foster family, they had visited an area called 'Hollywood.' Many people there spent much time adorning their flesh, and others came from miles around to worship these people that they called 'stars.' He smiled thinking about the stars up in the heavens and these so called 'stars', they were some of the homeliest people that he had ever seen. The sin that many had involved themselves in had brought some of the ugliest boils and sores upon their souls, equal to that infamous place called Sodom and Gomorrah.

Suddenly, in the midst of Adaiah's thoughts, the atmosphere of the room began to change.

Silencing his mind the angel waited, listening to heavenly words only an angel could hear. It was a call to attention. He stood up and vanished from the room.

In an instant he was in the heavens. Adaiah strode eagerly toward a gathering of angels. All were hovering, crowding, peering past one another to see Michael as he stood authoritatively at the head of a great silver table, his face turned as he talked quietly with his aide. The glorious Archangel's reflection shone clearly below him like a rainbow upon placid waters as he turned to face the room and motioned for attention with a sweep of his arm.

There were many other angels seated beside Adaiah, they too had been given command of the remnant of which his charge was a part. Each one was captain of a large fighting army of angels, and was assigned to one of these 'hidden ones.'

As Michael began to speak, Adaiah thought of how strong and powerful the Archangel was, and how special it was to be close to one who had served the King of Glory Himself. Michael's words were instructive and encouraging:

"The enemy is aware of all the activity in the heavens, and it is imperative that all fighting angels be on constant alert. The enemy is extremely subtle and he wants nothing more than to kill every part of the remnant. His greatest weapon is now within the church itself. Many false teachers have been raised up and even now are stealing the flock away from the freedom of the Gospel for which Christ gave up His own life. The church itself must be divided and the sheep separated from the goats. A new breed of leaders is about to come forth out of the remnant, who will lead the people into all truth. Along with this there will be a return of persecution to the saints. All the angels must be ready to follow the leading of the Spirit, allowing some to be martyred, and stealing some away from death until the time when the Father calls for their departure. It will begin small, but as the truth is being revealed, the Antichrist spirit within the religious system will attempt to crucify any who get in its path. Remember the Pharisees who came against the Son of God, for it is this same spirit at work even now in the world.

At all costs it is imperative that the remnant be guarded from this Antichrist spirit. Their training must be done in the wilderness of the Spirit. There are many pockets where the remnant can meet with other believers to worship, but even in these places the Antichrist could lay his deadly trappings. All angels must be ready to cause diversions and remove their charges from costly situations."

It was quite a speech that Michael gave and it had renewed the strength of Adaiah. The hardest part would be if the Father called for the death of his charge, Bilshan, to be allowed. He loved her so much and it was hard to tolerate the saints being put through torture. He remembered the stories that he had heard from the angels who had been at the crucifixion of Christ, and how they were held back from helping Him in any way. To many of them it had been the closest that they had ever come to having human tears and wailing. The hordes of hell were all around laughing and mocking the angels, spewing their black spittle of hate all over everything.

The angels had cried out to the Father to be allowed to rescue the Son from the shame of it. But the Father Himself had turned away from the Son and had left Him alone in that darkest hour of all time. Nothing had ever matched it in darkness and never would.

Then, gloriously, the resurrected Son of God brought freedom. The people that were brought out of Abraham's bosom and into the splendour of Heaven were many. Adaiah knew that he would have to concentrate upon the final outcome and not the current sufferings if he were to be able to stay by her side through all her trials. The angel made himself focus on that thought as he sped back to Bilshan's side.

Chapter Two

The sound seemed to be coming from a great distance, and yet it pulled at her. She felt so groggy, where was she anyway? It was like a big cave, and there was the sound of a heartbeat echoing through it. As another sound pulled her out of her sleep and the deep cave, she strained to keep the feeling of the heartbeat with her. The other sound was now yelling at her loud and clear, the ringing of the telephone.

As she awakened, first she glanced out the window to see if it was daylight yet. No, it was still dark, who would be calling at this hour. *What time is it anyway?* Susan spoke to herself. The clock said 2:53 A.M. in bright, bold letters, as she reached for the phone.

"Hello," she said groggily. On the other end of the line she could hear sobbing and crying. "Who's there?" She asked, feeling her stomach tighten as she spoke. "Susan! It's me, Karen," came the voice on the other end.

"Karen, are you all right?" Susan responded with concern, "What's the matter?" Again the crying started and Susan could not understand what Karen was saying. "Slow down, Karen, I can't understand you, and I can't help if you don't try to get a grip on yourself." She was feeling a panic slowly rise up in her chest causing her to catch her breath with her words.

Finally, Karen blurted out, "Susan! I really need you to come over right now. I can't say this on the phone." Karen began sobbing wildly again at this point.

"Of course Karen, I'll be over as soon as I can, will you be okay til I get there?" Susan replied, not feeling very sure of herself and not knowing if she really wanted to go over there. The dread that was coming upon her was different from anything that she had ever felt. But the commitment she felt to her friend was greater than her fears. "I don't know, but I'll try. Just hurry, okay." Cried Karen.

As she hung up the phone, Susan could not help feeling apprehensive. Karen was one of her closest friends, she had a roommate that she shared her apartment with named Tiffany, who was also Susan's friend. The three of them often did things together, like going to the mall or a movie.

She liked both of them because they were so easygoing and brought a lightness to her often too serious thoughts.

She hurriedly dressed and headed out for her car, hoping that it would start right up. It was an old, second hand car that she had bought right after she graduated from high school, and even then it did not hold much promise to last long. The car started right up and as she put it in gear, heading for Karen's house, the possibilities of what lie ahead made her clutch the steering wheel a little too tight, and drive a little too fast.

As she drove along, the remembrance of the dream she had been awakened out of came to her.

What was that heartbeat about? Why do I feel so needful to know who this strange heart belongs to? Surely it was her own heart that she had heard beating in the dream, but somehow she knew it wasn't. Again she had that feeling that someone out there was with her, someone or something was trying to reach her, and she felt the pull toward this unknown entity.

Finally, she rounded the corner to where her friends' apartment was. She gasped as she came close. There were two police cars and an ambulance also. Her heart sank within her as she knew that all the attention was focussed upon Karen and Tiffany's apartment.

As she tried to enter the hallway to number 223, where they lived, a police officer gently grabbed her arm.

"I'm sorry Miss, you can't go in there," he said as he tried to redirect her. But at that moment, Karen saw her and came running out of the doorway. "Oh Susan, I'm so glad you are here!" Karen cried as she clung to Susan. The police officer stood back to let them go by. She and Karen walked toward the doorway, but as they did, a strong feeling that something dreadful had happened came over Susan, and she wanted to turn and run. She felt her heart drop as she saw the blood on the floor, and reached her hands out for something to steady herself on. She fell back toward a small book table in the doorway as her stomach heaved slightly, her head felt dizzy as she tried to catch her breath. *Just breathe,* she told herself, *just keep breathing.* Finally, as she steadied herself, she looked up at Karen and asked, "what has happened here?"

Karen was sobbing softly and saying something about not knowing, and not seeing the signs.

Susan was unable to get any more out of Karen when a stretcher went past her with Tiffany lying motionless upon it. She had blood all over her sweatshirt, but her wrists were bandaged up and Susan began to get a picture of what had happened.

"Did Tiffany try to kill herself?" She asked Karen, whispering as if not wanting to say the words out loud for the fear of their meaning.

Karen could only nod in agreement, and then she started to cry again, sobbing loudly. "I should have seen the signs, I should have been home earlier, It's all my fault."

Susan tried to soothe Karen and calm her down. Then the police officer came back in after helping to put Tiffany onto the ambulance. Susan met with him and quietly asked if Tiffany was going to die.

"She's in serious condition, and she's lost a lot of blood." He gently took Susan's arm directing her over toward Karen and spoke compassionately. "They will do all that they can to help her. She will be at Memorial Hospital, you can check on her after you get her friend here calmed down." His eyes were soft with concern and understanding. Then he turned and headed out the door joining the other officer working on a report. It became quiet so suddenly. Susan still felt dazed. She looked around the room with unbelieving eyes, her heart thumping loudly in her ears, the desire to run still upon her. Then she heard Karen again, and turned to see her friend fall down hard on the couch in sobs.

Susan sat down with Karen and continued to hold her, trying to keep her calm. She tried to imagine Tiffany, their light-hearted friend, wanting to commit suicide, but it just didn't make any sense. It had only been a few days since they were last together, and Tiffany seemed fine then. Or was she? Susan remembered a conversation with Tiffany in which she spoke of applying to get into a Nursing program at a local college. Apparently Tiffany's family had high hopes of their daughter becoming a Nurse. Tiffany seemed unsure of the decision, and felt that her heart was not really in it. She stated that she felt uncertain about the future, and how she would fit into it. Susan had not encouraged the conversation any, mostly because she really enjoyed the easygoing banter that was common between them. She had lightly laughed at Tiffany and said she should do whatever made her feel good, not to worry about her parents. "Just do your own thing," was what she had said.

Now she was feeling a bit guilty herself. She had not cared enough to listen to her friend when she needed help. Then she thought of that mysterious heartbeat that she had heard in her dream, even now she could hear the echo of it. Was that what Tiffany was trying to sound out the other night? Was her heart crying to be heard and understood? How could she ever learn to listen to unseen entities out there, if she could not even hear the voice of her of a close friend?

She wanted to hit herself for getting off into these strange thoughts. But instead she focussed on calming her friend, Karen. First thing in the morning they would go to the hospital and see Tiffany. But for now to clean up the mess and get Karen off to bed.

Adaiah was there, he had flown beside her all the way, and even now as he heard the thoughts that Bilshan was thinking, he smiled to himself saying, *very good, she is ready to have her heart revealed.* He knew that this was the first step that all believers must take to come face to face with the truth. She would need to have all her motives exposed, and she would need to see that she had nothing to offer anyone outside of the Truth. Of course, she had not yet met the Truth, or the Spirit of Truth, but it was close. Tomorrow, in the hospital, there would be a man in the waiting room who would begin to open her eyes to her need for the Truth. In fact, now it was time to go and visit that man, to prepare him for the 'chance' meeting that he was to be at, where a seed of God would be planted and the girl would become aware of the True Life that was available to her.

Susan felt restless and uncomfortable. She wanted to deny the thoughts that were forcing themselves upon her. *You should have cared more about your friend and her needs. Why didn't you listen when she needed you?*

What kind of person ignores a friend who is reaching out for help anyway? On and on her thoughts went and she fought the feelings of failure that were closing in on her.

Karen had calmed down and was sleeping on the couch next to her. Yet even in her sleep, a soft moan of pain was coming out with each breath. Susan knew that Karen was also feeling as if she had been the cause of Tiffany's troubles.

Chapter Three

His prayer time had extended late into the night again, here it was after three in the morning. Paul wondered how time could fly by so fast. He sat back on the floor cross legged and thought of how much he would rather be praying than anything else. It seemed that he only tolerated the rest of his life out of necessity more than desire. Of course, he loved his family. His wife and two daughters were a great joy to him. But always there was that call to come away in solitude, and it seemed to be even stronger lately.

The church where they had been attending had all but rejected him. He knew that he would never be able to fit into the same mould that other men seemed to fit into. He could not help his strong emotions about the Ancient book and its words, and whenever he stood up in church to share the portion of writing that was on his heart, he would become so involved in its words that the intensity of his voice would cause his listeners to grimace. It was not his intention to be so serious. He was just that way. To be any different would be to try and change all that he was created to be. He knew that he was not capable of having these intense feelings on his own. They came upon him, usually in the midst of the reading. He would catch his breath, and a look of soul-piercing intensity would come into his eyes, then tears would well up. How could he be any different? To do so would be to deny the presence of the Spirit that he longed for each day and night in his prayers.

Paul knew that he must face the rejection and accept that it would happen. He saw it in the Ancient book and knew that there were others who had spoken its truth and been rejected. He had come to a place where he would no longer seek the acceptance of his peers, but only the acceptance of his Heavenly Father who meant everything to him.

Paul's wife, Janna, lay awake in bed. After tossing and turning to the point that she had to remake the bed, she finally gave herself over to the troubling thoughts that were beckoning her.

She was back in church on Sunday, and the conversation replayed itself in her mind. Her friends were trying to persuade her that Paul was acting different for the attention that he got, that he really wasn't as sincere as he would have folks believe. Janna thought long and hard on these words. It was true that Paul had once been driven by insecurity. He had been abused as a child and as he grew there were many obstacles for him to overcome. She had seen him move out of insecurity before and knew that it was very possible. Yet as she had watched and listened to him, she knew that he was a changed man from any insecurities of the past. Paul had truly become more secure in his calling and less in need of approval from others. He was a passionate man who loved the Ancient book, and who loved prayer. He was not like other men in that he didn't really care for sports, or the things that other men did. It was not that he wanted to be that way. He was made that way for some reason. Paul lived for God, and he took his life as a believer very seriously.

Janna remembered the cruel treatment that was meted out by certain people who didn't know Paul, they seemed to judge him without even trying to get to know him. If fact, it seemed that many of them had tried to forget that Paul and Janna even existed rather than to befriend and get to know one another. No one called anymore, meetings were held and they were not invited. Promises had been broken. When they had first come to the church, the Pastor had encouraged Paul that he would take him under his wing in training for the ministry, but when Paul had failed to conform to what was expected, he was cast aside as if a rag doll and another 'more promising' man had been put in that role.

At first, Janna had felt so betrayed that she wanted to run away and never go back. But Paul had convinced her that it was best that they stay and encourage any others who might fall through the cracks as they had. And sure enough, a couple who was suffering from rejection had come to them and they had become fast friends. This relationship had brought some much needed encouragement to her and she was thankful that the Father was showing her His love by bringing new friends into her life. Paul also reminded her that God never closes one door without opening another, and that she should keep her eyes on the Lord and not on the situations around her.

Janna's eyes became heavy and sleep threatened to take over. As she gave herself over to the steady breathing and lulling quiet of the atmosphere she wondered if Paul would be up again the whole night. As she drifted off, she prayed that the Father would bless her husband and use him to bless others.

Paul was getting ready to go to bed when something in the room began to change. He felt a brightness, an electrifying something that he couldn't put his finger on. It was as if the room itself were aglow with some strange, golden light. His mind felt sharp and clear, and he wondered that the Holy Spirit Himself were here in this place.

Then, suddenly, in front of him appeared a man. Well not quite like a real man, this man looked perfect, and bigger than any man he had ever met. There was a bright light about the man and an unearthly sense that caused fear to well up within Paul as he fell face forward onto the carpet. His first thought was that he might be dying, for his heart gripped him and he felt the puny existence of his flesh surrounding him. He felt very corrupted, and somehow sinful in the presence of such an awesome being.

Adaiah had only had a few contacts with the physical realm, and each time the person had fallen before him as if in worship. He knew that it was at first a shock for a man to come in contact with an angelic being and that he must be patient. He could not help but be bothered at the sight of one of the creation, that the Son himself was planning to marry, bow before him. The angel started toward the man and put his hand out to help him up, saying "do not be afraid, I am only a messenger of the Most High God."

The man, ever so slowly, began to peek out from under his arm. Adaiah looked at him with the most reassuring kindness and encouraged him to get up, motioning with his hand that there was nothing to fear.

The angel smiled as he thought of how frail the flesh was, and what joy people had when they received their new bodies. He loved to watch the incoming saints because they were always so in awe of the heavenly bodies that they found themselves in. Often they had seen the destruction of their flesh and carried the fear that it would be in sad shape, only to realize that the flesh was of the earth and returned to its original form of dust when the spirit left it. *Bad enough to have to live in it on the earth, let alone take it to heaven*, the angel smiled as he thought. The new, glorious bodies were uncorrupted by the stains of sin and worked to a full capacity. But he could not explain this to one who lived in the flesh, he could only hope to instill the idea that the flesh was not worth saving.

Adaiah waited patiently as the man got his wits about him and sat up. He could see that the man was wondering if this was real. The angel watched as the man rubbed his eyes, and pinched himself hard only to yell "Ouch." Then, as reality struck, the man focussed on the angel and the two sat watching each other, waiting for words to be spoken.

Paul slowly got up and looked at the angel. *Could it be? An angel was visiting him.* He wished he knew what to say to the angel, but he felt speechless. So he stood and waited.

The angel looked at him intently and began to speak. Paul felt shocked that the angel would speak as if it were a natural thing. The words that came forth were instructions.

"This is an important mission. You must go to Memorial Hospital at 10:30 a.m. Go straight to the waiting room and sit in the gold chair in the northwest corner of the room. You will be alone in the room for a short time, so make sure that you shut off the TV before you sit down. Take the Ancient book with you, for you will need to refer to it. Shortly thereafter a young woman with brown hair and hazel eyes will come in looking rather distraught. You are to motion her to come over and sit by you. Her name is Susan Jones and her friend, Tiffany, has died of committing suicide. You are to tell her that you know who she is and that the Father has sent you to her. The answers about the mysteries of creation are to be revealed to her. Tell her that the heart she heard beating in her dream is the Fathers' heart toward her. He is ready to make Himself known to her. She will listen to you when you say these words, but she will also cry out that she has caused the death of her friend and she could not possibly worthy to be sought by any such 'Father.' This will be the cry of repentance that will open the door for the true gospel of forgiveness to be preached to her. You must lead her to the Lamb of God and His atonement for her sin."

"Do not tell her anything else, for her training will be different from anything you know of. After she prays to receive the King of Glory, Jesus Christ the Messiah into her heart, you must encourage her to come over to your home and meet your wife. She will soon afterwards meet with me, and she must be prepared for the encounter."

As the angel spoke, it seemed that the words were ingrained into Paul's mind as if the angel were not only speaking to him, but was somehow speaking within him. It amazed Paul at the simplicity of the message, as if it should have been something more important somehow. Then he realized his thoughts and wondered at himself, what could be more important than the salvation of a lost person?

Adaiah was watching the man intently to be sure that he understood all the instructions that were being given to him. Since the Angel also had the ability to understand the thoughts of man, he knew that Paul was indeed taking his mission seriously. It was now time for him to depart, and he looked at the man and spoke into his mind that he would be leaving now. But just as he was disappearing, the man lunged at him and cried out, "Bless me, you must bless me first!"

The man was holding on tight, but the angel knew that he could easily slip from his grasp, yet the Holy Spirit spoke that he should not, but instead should bless him. The angel put out his hand upon Pauls' head and spoke, "You are Anaiah, for Yahweh has answered you, and you have received His blessing."

Then as suddenly as he had appeared, the angel vanished into thin air.

Chapter Four

Susan awoke with a start, it took a moment to take in all that had happened the night before. She looked around the room, seeing that she was not home and that it was not a dream, she was still in Karen and Tiffany's apartment, and Karen was sleeping soundly on the couch next to her. She must have dozed off after Karen had settled down. She wondered how Tiffany was doing.

As Susan started to move around, Karen woke up startled. She looked around and then cried out, "Oh how I wish it were just a bad dream."

At that moment the shrill sound of the telephone disrupted the quiet of the room, shaking Susan out of her thoughts. Karen reached over to answer it. Susan decided to get up and find some coffee, she didn't have enough sleep to face the day ahead, that she knew. As she was snooping about the kitchen looking for the coffee, Karen came in and said that Tiffany's Mom had just phoned and they would be coming over to get her and bring her to the hospital.

Karen looked pale and shaky, her voice was muted as she spoke. "They said that Tiffany has not regained consciousness. They don't think that she will make it Susan."

Karen searched Susan's face as if looking for a thread of hope, and finding none she turned and walked out of the room.

Susan felt herself go limp. She grabbed the table to steady herself and cried out "Why!"at the top of her lungs. She wanted to say something as Karen walked away, but the words would not come. She had nothing to offer Karen, no hope, no answers, nothing. Finally she found her voice and spoke numbly. "I'll follow in my car."

Susan finally managed to find the coffee, and made it twice as strong in hopes of receiving some extra energy for what lie ahead.

Later, as she drove to the hospital, Susan couldn't help thinking of all that had taken place, and how she had never before faced the possible death of a loved one. She had never known a family, and had always felt sort of sterile and protected from feeling the pains and joys of family relationships. She felt that her life was about to take a turn, and there was no way for her to know how to prepare for it. How could she deal with this? What could she do now, it was too late for action, for communication with a girl she called 'friend' and yet had not listened to her real needs. Susan felt desperate to change things, yet helpless and inadequate. What could she do?

Adaiah was there with her, flying along beside her car. He knew her thoughts and smiled to himself as he agreed that a big change was about to come to her life. It was to him, the thing that he had waited for so long. He loved the Father and His Son, and the thought that she was about to be introduced to them caused a thrill that had already brought a praise song to his lips. In fact, he could also hear his army singing as they followed close by, ever on the alert. He knew that many of the angels and also the great cloud of witnesses would also join in the celebration of the salvation of a soul.

Paul was up and dressed by 7:30 a.m., he was almost impatient for the time to come when he could begin his drive over to the hospital. He had not even tried to tell Janna of his experience, he was not sure that he could tell it yet, he still felt speechless. He had the Ancient book in his bag and a list of certain texts that would be helpful in leading this young woman to the cross.

He thrilled at the thought of it. God had blessed him, and now he was to be an instrument in bringing another sheep, like himself, into the sheepfold. He thought of the rejection from the church that had befallen him, and he smiled, knowing that it was true, God never closes a door without opening another one.

Adaiah, still singing and flying alongside Bilshan as she drove to the hospital, wasn't expecting the sudden change in the spiritual atmosphere. The sky around them had taken on the eerie red glow that could only mean one thing. Just as he was sensing the change, his chief officer, Edrei, suddenly came alongside.

Edrei's name meant 'mighty,' and that he was. Adaiah was glad that Edrei had been assigned to him, he was trustworthy and of all the fighting angels, Adaiah knew that Edrei had a special sense of what the enemy was up to.

Edrei spoke. "It's a trap. There is a car up ahead and the demonic presence on the man in the driver's seat undeniable. I feel that he may try something with our charge. Is it possible to create a diversion?"

Adaiah thought for a moment and then smiled at Edrei. "I know just the thing." Then he swiftly headed into the engine of Bilshan's car.

"Oh no!" Cried Susan, as her car sputtered to a stop. "Not now! Not here! And please not today!" The car had stalled as she found just enough power to pull it off the road. Over and over she tried to get it to restart, but the engine only coughed and finally the battery quit trying.

Now what? She thought to herself. Karen was too far ahead in the other car to notice that Susan was not following them and there wasn't a telephone in sight. She got out and came around to the hood of the car, opening it she found that the engine was throwing off some steam, and since she knew absolutely nothing about car motors, she slammed the hood back down and stood there.

"I guess its time to walk," she spoke to no one in particular. Grabbing her purse, she started off for the long trek to the hospital.

"Now for part B of our plan." Adaiah spoke to Edrei. "I'm going over to see Anaiah, and give him the change of plans." Once again Adaiah disappeared and Edrei was left with their charge, Bilshan.

Paul was finally in his car and on the road. He thought of how his poor wife had looked at him this morning when he had tried to explain things, but the words just wouldn't come. He had even stuttered, which was something that he never did. She had tried to feel his head to see if maybe he had a fever or something, so he knew that she was very concerned.

When he got ready to leave, he simply said that he had a mission from God, and when he came home he might be bringing company, so she should be prepared. She just stared at him when he left. Paul smiled to himself as he thought of his wife. *She'll be okay. She trusts God.*

Then, as Paul was driving, he felt his car light up with that same presence that he had felt the night before when the angel had appeared to him. Just as suddenly, he saw the angel again, and it was all he could do to maintain the steering wheel of the car as he drove.

There was the same angel, sitting in the passenger seat right next to him. Paul took a deep breath and blew it out slowly, thinking to himself. *Get a grip. This is what you have wanted, to have contact with the spiritual realm, so get used to it.* Then he turned to the Angel and smiled and tried to speak, but he was rendered speechless again.

Adaiah smiled as he looked on the man and heard his thoughts. He was indeed doing very well with these heavenly encounters.

He then spoke to the man. "I am known as Adaiah, meaning 'Yahweh has adorned', and I am head overseer of the girl I spoke to you about last night."

It was good to speak with man. To be close to one of the beloved of His Master was always a treat for the angel. He knew that one of the reasons for his own creation was to be a servant to these who were created in His Majesty's image. Adaiah saw that the man wanted to speak to him, so he looked at him and spoke into his mind that he could understand his thoughts and it would be better than trying to speak out loud.

Paul was taken aback. Did he really hear what he thought he heard? He looked over at the angel, and the angel smiled and nodded 'yes' in agreement. Then the angel spoke into his mind again.

"There has been a change of plans. I want you to turn around up ahead at the next intersection.

You are about to pick up the girl that I spoke to you about. When you see her, pull over and ask her if she needs a ride. I will be here with you in the car, but you will not be able to see me. You will hear me speak though, as long as you permit it. I cannot be heard by anyone who resists hearing me, just as the Holy Spirit can be disregarded by man when He speaks."

Paul thought of how often that he had heard that still, small voice of the Spirit in his heart. He had many times just passed over it as though it were a noise in the wind. But he knew in his heart of hearts that it was the Spirit, because many times when he had heard the voice, it had been in relation to guidance in his life. He thought of a time recently when he was upset with his wife about something he couldn't even remember now. The voice had said to go over and hug her and say that he was sorry for being inconsiderate of her feelings. But he had wanted to hold on to his anger, so he brushed the words aside like he would an out of place hair on his head, without giving it a moments thought. How he wished that he would listen more and think less.

The angel was smiling at him and nodding in agreement. Then the thought came into Paul's mind, that this was the wisdom that came from above. It would be wise for him to heed these thoughts, for the Spirit had much more wisdom to impart to Paul and was patiently waiting for him to obey the first, small impressions. Then the Spirit could increase Paul's insight.

Then, as they were driving along, Paul saw a young woman walking along the right side of the road. He wondered if she were the one that he was to pick up. The angel answered his thoughts, *Yes, she is the one.* Paul pulled the car over and got out, he was nervous as he thought of what he was to say. He felt that his life was never going to be the same again.

Chapter Five

Meanwhile, in a small prison cell about 150 miles north, a young man by the name of David was sitting alone on his cot. He had been to the library early that morning and had come across a strange book hidden way in the back behind some more popular reading material. He had heard of the book, and that many referred to it as an ancient book with writings dating back several thousand years. When he had first seen the book, he wasn't very interested in it because he knew that it was related to some type of religion, and he was not interested in that sort of thing. Yet something about the book seemed to reach out to him though, and he found himself unable to resist its pull. So he checked it out from the librarian and brought it back to his cell with him.

Now, as he sat fingering the worn pages of the book, his thoughts began to drift off again to the same thoughts that had tormented him for the past seven years, the reason for his imprisonment.

It was a day like any other day, but one that would tragically alter the course of his life. He was newly married, about six months previously, and he adored his wife. She was a fun-loving, and voracious, with the energy to try and live each day to its fullest. She reminded him of some wild, exotic islander with her long, jet black hair and her tan skin. He was so in love that it was hard for him to concentrate on his job as a computer programmer. He would often find himself wanting to leave work and come home to surprise her with plans for an afternoon getaway. And on this particular day that is exactly what he did.

When he pulled up in the driveway of their modest little home, he was surprised to see his best friends' truck parked in his driveway. Johnny was like a brother to him, they had graduated high school together and stayed buddies as the years went by. Often, he and his wife would meet with Johnny (and whoever his latest fling was), and they would go water skiing, or hiking or whatever caught their fancy at the time. He didn't think it was too unusual for Johnny's truck to be there, because he bounded into the house ready to surprise her anyway.

How he wished now that he had been suspicious and slowed down, maybe he would have been able to get his emotions under control and not done what he did. That was not what happened. He walked in the door, and there they were. The two of them together in the passion of lovemaking was more than he could tolerate. He had stopped and stood there speechless, looking from friend to wife, and back again. Looking for words, for reason, for anything to grab hold of. But there was nothing, no sense, no understanding. Then the rage had come, as he looked to and fro and began to understand the meaning of their togetherness, his mind exploded in rage. He couldn't see clearly, his head spun, and he felt as if he would pass out from the heat boiling in his head. Then his body took over. He had run wildly past them, into his bedroom and gotten his gun. He was out of control, and when he had returned, David's so called friend was making haste toward his truck when David shot those fatal shots into Johnny's back.

Everything else was a blur. The trial, the sentence, and even the divorce papers that his wife's attorney had presented him on his way to the penitentiary. His life had ended that day, never to be the same again. Prison life was horrible. He spent as much time alone as he was allowed. He kept his eyes to the floor whenever he was in the presence of the other convicts, and for the past seven years, he had managed to stay out of trouble. He knew that he was to be up for parole soon, and that he would probably be released, but to what? How could he ever live in the world again? He had no one. No family, no wife, no one. At least here he had a routine to follow. But what would it be like out there.

He was a convicted murderer. He would carry the record with him the rest of his life. What hope would he have of finding a job with his record? In addition he knew that the computer industry had changed and all his knowledge was outdated. The prison had a few old computers, but none of the new technology that would be required for him to know if he were to obtain employment.

He sighed to himself as he looked at the ancient book in his hands. *Oh well*, he thought, *I guess I'll just lose myself in another book. This one looks like it will take the rest of the year to read judging by the size of it and the small print.*

He opened the book to the first page and began to read.

Chapter Six

As Paul got out of his car and came toward Susan, he could sense the Angel's presence with him, but he could not see him. It did help his confidence though, for he was not the type who picked up strange girls and offered them rides. As he came near to the girl, he called out to her.

"Hey, do you need some help?", he said with as much sincerity as he could, he wanted to keep from seeming strange to her. Just then the thought came to him to say that he had noticed a car stranded along the highway a little way back and that he thought it might belong to her.

"I saw a car pulled over back there, and then I see you walking and I thought that you might be having trouble," he spoke, feeling better about the whole situation.

Susan turned and looked at the man, she saw that he seemed sincere in his desire to help her, and since she did not relish the thought of walking three more miles to the hospital, she spoke to him.

"Yes, that was my car. It just quit on me, and I don't know anything about motors so I just left it and started walking." She looked closely at the man while she spoke. He was small and stout looking. He reminded her of a mill worker or a logger or something by the style of his dress. He wore blue jeans and a flannel shirt. She also saw that he was wearing a wedding ring on his finger.

"Well I'm not much of a mechanic either, but could I give you a lift somewhere and maybe get a tow truck for your car?" Paul responded. This wasn't as hard as he thought it would be.

"Yes, that would be very helpful. I need to get to Memorial Hospital as quickly as possible. I was planning to walk all the way, but a ride would be much easier and quicker." She walked over toward his car as he held the passenger door open for her.

"Oh, by the way, my name is Paul Chandler. I'm a local handyman around here. I live over on Highway 16." Paul was trying to make her feel as comfortable as he could. She seemed like a nice girl. He was probably old enough to be her father.

As they drove along, making small talk, Adaiah was sitting in the back seat unseen. He spoke into Paul's thoughts that he should just make small talk and drive her to the hospital, then he should follow the plan as it was given the night before. At that moment, Edrei appeared next to him.

"It looks good out there. It was just as I thought, the car that the evil presence was attached to pulled out at the same time that we would have passed by. The driver did not look before he pulled out, it would have been a terrible wreck. He did cause the car that was behind our charge to swerve and miss having a collision. But the timing was perfect for our charge had her car been there."

Adaiah thought of how many times they had done these same type of maneuvers. He thought of the reading in the Ancient book that said, "He will give His Angels charge over them, lest they hit their foot against a rock." Chuckling he spoke to Edrei, "rocks would be easier than these fast cars they are using nowadays."

Smiling, Edrei agreed. Then the Warrior angel disappeared back into the ranks. The car with Adaiah's charge was just now pulling up to the hospital. Susan turned to Paul and spoke. "Can I pay you or something? I really appreciate the ride!" But Paul shook his head 'no' and responded that he was glad he could help. Susan got out of the car and headed into the hospital.

It was 10:20 when Paul parked the car and headed for the waiting room that he had been told about the night before. He walked in and found it to be empty just as the angel had predicted. He walked over to the TV which was blaring with one of those crazy talk shows that he abhorred and gladly shut it off. He went over to the gold chair that was sitting in the northwest corner of the room. Looking at his watch, he saw that it was 10:32, *6 more minutes to wait*, he thought to himself. He pulled out the Ancient book and began to refresh himself in the material that he had chosen and waited.

Susan had entered the Intensive Care Unit where she had been told that Tiffany was located. As she walked in, she saw Karen and Tiffany's mom holding each other and crying. Tiffany's dad was sitting in a chair close by with a stunned look on his face. Susan felt her stomach tighten, as her heart began to beat wildly. Just as she came up to them, Karen looked up and saw Susan. She motioned Susan toward the room where Tiffany had been. Susan walked toward the door.

There lay Tiffany, white and still, lifeless she knew. A nurse was getting ready to pull the sheet over Tiffany's face when she noticed that Susan had come into the room.

"Was she your friend?" The nurse questioned her gently.

Susan looked into the compassionate eyes of the nurse and could only nod. "Is she gone?" she spoke motioning toward Tiffany.

The nurse walked over toward Susan and put her arm out to steady her. "She never regained consciousness. She lost too much blood by the time she was found. I'm so sorry."

Susan started to back away, crying out "No, it can't be. Not Tiffany. Why?" She headed out the door. But when she came out there was Tiffany's mom and dad looking so distraught. Susan turned and ran away, as she ran she saw a sign leading toward the waiting room, she hoped that it would be empty. She needed to cry, and wanted to scream.

Chapter Seven

Paul looked at his watch. It was 10:38. He closed the Ancient book and left it on his lap as he looked up toward the entrance of the waiting room. Susan had just entered the room, and she was standing there staring at Paul, her face drained of all color. Paul swallowed hard and told himself to trust in the Lord, it would all work out. He smiled at Susan with a sympathetic smile and motioned for her to come and sit by him.

Susan had stalled when she entered the room as she saw the man who had given her a ride sitting there in the corner of the room. At first she wanted to turn around and find a private place to run to. Yet she couldn't understand the lure she felt toward the man. It was as if a light was illuminating the area surrounding him and she felt so drawn that she could not resist. She walked slowly toward him.

Paul felt the Holy Spirit within him surge with anointing. He knew that he would become a vessel for the Spirit to work through as this wayward soul approached him. He was thankful that the Spirit was in control, and he felt himself relax and yield to the flow.

"Susan," Paul spoke, "I've been waiting for you. I've been sent to you today by the Father. He has been calling you." He stopped and took a deep breath. How hard this must be for her, losing a close friend was something he had never dealt with and he knew only God could comfort her now. He felt his eyes tear up at the thought of her pain, the compassion welled up with him. "I know that you are in shock right now because of your friends' death," at this he sighed and looked into her eyes, feeling a strength not his own he reached out his hand reassuringly, he spoke softly, his words soothing and comforting, "but the Father can help you through it all. He loves you so much, in fact, He would not withhold His own Son from you to show you His love."

Susan just stared at the man, she felt so drawn to his comfort and compassion, his eyes showed a love and concern that was unnatural for a stranger.

"How do you know my name? I did not tell it to you. Who are you?" She felt a mixture of fear and curiosity at the man's strange words about a Father. "And how do you know that my friend has just died?" How could he know these things? She still felt the light that was surrounding this man, and he spoke of something that was somehow related to her search, this she knew. She felt as though she were a drowning person and this man held the only hope for her survival, he held the life saver and she somehow wanted to grasp it.

"I am a follower of the Way and I have been told that you are a seeker of this Truth that can answer all your questions. I was told that He came to you in a dream the other night. You heard His heart beating for you. The cave that you were in represents the darkness that you dwell in, but He can bring you to the Light of His Truth, His Son Jesus Christ. I have the Ancient book here and I can show you what He has for you." Paul was amazed at the confidence that he felt as he spoke, he knew that it was of the Spirit of God and that Jesus spoke with the same boldness when

He was on the earth. It was good to know that God is faithful at the time needed.

Susan had heard of this Ancient book and had met a few of these followers before, but she had never met someone who spoke with such authority and knowledge of it before. It was almost as if the man actually knew the author of the book. Even though a part of her wanted to run away from the craziness of it all, she could not resist the pull she felt at wanting to hear all that he spoke of. Slowly she walked to the nearest chair and sat down. After taking a deep breath and letting out all of her need to cry for the moment, she looked at the man who so boldly spoke to her and nodded her head.

"I want to hear of these things. I don't understand how you know of my dream and these things about me, so tell me about the Ancient book and this Father that you speak of."

Adaiah was sitting close by, unseen by the physical world. He smiled as Anaiah, or Paul as he was known to the outer world, spoke to his charge. Also sitting close by was Taralah, the Angel who had been assigned to Paul. Taralah was of the order of Angels who served those saints who would be given a special anointing of power for their ministry on the earth. Adaiah himself was of the order of Angels who brought treasures of God's wisdom to certain vessels so chosen. Both Angels had great respect for one another, knowing that each ministry was of great value, these and many more, to the coming times. Even at this moment Taralah was ministering his power to Paul as he spoke. Light was given to the words that Paul spoke bringing a special illumination that caused even the simplest of minds to understand.

Adaiah thought to himself about the love the Father had for these fragile beings. Truth was never hidden from those who searched for it, and yet there were so many who settled for false teaching, not willing to go beyond the crowd that they were trying to please. The problem of pride and its outworking of insecurity was the major source of the false teachings that seemed to pervade these times. If only this chosen race could see the unique calling on each of their lives and the willingness of the Spirit to give each of them his own portion of Truth.

The angel sighed deeply as he thought of how hard they were fighting against the Antichrist spirit that captured the hearts and minds of so many. Numerous teachers were guilty of keeping these precious ones from discovering their true callings. The Antichrist spirit had brought such a heavy burden to the flock. Often many were taught that they must be like their teachers, and these teachers exalted in their own callings. This caused many of the diverse callings to simply disappear from the ministry all together.

Adaiah knew that things were about to change. The church would again become what she was destined to be. A bride without spot or wrinkle, each member fitting and perfect with a unity of purpose and calling that made each and every part of her 'makeup' special.

Paul was intently sharing the gospel message. He opened the Ancient book and spoke of how the creation had left the 'One' for whom it had been created. His words flowed with the plan of Life and salvation, and Susan listened with all of her heart, the tears flowing freely as she wept over the love that was being shown to her. How could God care so much? It was such a mystery to her, and the simplicity of it was almost too much for comprehension. That God loved her at all was unthinkable, and then the thought that He sent His own Son to take her place and suffer her death was incredible. Then she remembered Tiffany, and again the hopelessness came at her, she could not help feeling guilty and sad over the loss of her friend, and she spoke of it to Paul.

"Why did Tiffany have to die? Why couldn't she have received this Life you speak of? I know that she would have if she had only known. It just isn't right," Susan sobbed as she realized that her friend had probably never known the Truth and what He had done for her. Her pain was severe as she realized that this Truth had been kept from them, from her friends and so many people who needed life, hope, and help.

"I never want to see another person leave this world without knowing the Truth, they need to know, Paul" she exclaimed pulling at his arm. "I want to know Him. I can see now that my whole life has been waiting for the day when I would become His. Help me pray to Him. Show me how. I want His blood to cover me. I want this Life that you speak of. I'm miserable and wretched without Him. Please Paul, you must show me the Way!"

Adaiah smiled as he knelt on the floor beside his charge Bilshan, she was coming home.

Chapter Eight

J anna and the girls were just ready to put supper on the table when they heard a car pull up in the driveway. Joy, their oldest daughter, ran to the window to see who it was. "Mom, its dad and there is a lady with him," she hollered.

Janna looked up as Paul and the stranger entered the room. The so called 'Lady' really wasn't much more than a girl and Janna felt an immediate liking toward her.

"Hi, I'm Janna, Paul's wife, and these are our daughters, Joy and Katherine." Janna reached out her hand in a friendly gesture. "Would you like to join us for dinner? We were just sitting down?"

Susan looked around the cozy home and felt the warmth that was offered. She immediately felt the invitation was sincere. Janna seemed to be of a genuine type, and Susan felt a pull toward getting to know this matronly sort of woman. She smiled at Janna warmly and said, "I'd love to join you. Are you sure that I won't inconvenience you?", she felt humbled and honored to be invited to such a lovely table.

"Oh no, it is no trouble at all. We love to have company join us for meals. But let me warn you, we are a talkative bunch and love to chatter as we eat. We always look forward to breaking bread together and the communion of each other." Janna took Susan by the hand and led her gently toward the dining room.

The dinner was wonderful, simple, but very pleasant, Susan thought. The longer that she was around this family the more that she liked them. Joy and Katherine were little treasures to be around, they liked Susan and proceeded to show her all their toys and anything else that would bring attention to them. Susan basked in the pleasant atmosphere of the family, and it seemed that her pain at the loss of her friend was abated for the time being. The most marvelous thing about this family was the evident love that they all had for the Heavenly Father. He was often the subject of conversation, but not in some religious way, rather as though He were actually present in the room. In fact, it seemed that these people really lived what they professed. It was demonstrated by the way they spoke to each other, and how they considered others more important than themselves. Paul had told her that they often studied the teachings in the Ancient book and tried to live by them, and that the prayer they so often prayed was that His kingdom would come into the earthen vessels that they saw themselves as. Paul had spoken of the Ancient book so much today that it had put a hunger in Susan to study its words for herself. She had inquired as to where she might find her own copy of the book, but Paul had graciously given her his copy saying that he could share with his wife.

Adaiah was with Susan as usual, and later that night, after she had arrived home, he was ready to minister his light to her. His purpose as her Angel at this time would be to encourage her silently to read the Ancient book. The Holy Spirit was even now within her to illuminate the words as she read them, and he was sent now as a ministering Angel to this precious saint of God. He smiled as his ministering light went forth toward his charge, sighing deeply he spoke aloud to the invisible presence of the Spirit of God.

"It is always such a pleasure to serve Your chosen ones, my Lord. How I long for the time when they will be reunited with us in the fullness of all the realms. They are so fragile in these earthly abodes that they must dwell in. They have so little understanding of how You will rectify all human suffering at the end of the age. They try so hard to hold on to this fragile life and to apply all the words in the Ancient book in ways that simply are not meant to be. I pray for this one, that she will be free of the bondage of her flesh and able to receive the Truth beyond the fragile walls of her human understanding." The angel listened for the response of the Spirit. Quietly he nodded his head in agreement and then spoke again.

"Of course. You are right. She will have to bear in her flesh the seed of Adam until the fullness of the seed of Christ can take root. When that which is perfect has come, then she will no longer see through a glass darkly. And yet my Lord, will she stumble in darkness? Or perhaps You will avail more of Yourself to this one. What is her purpose? To what measure will her talents be?" The angel bowed low as he spoke. The desire to be filled with the presence of the Spirit was his one purpose in creation, to worship and to be filled. He could not help but desire filling for his charge. Again he listened as the Spirit spoke quietly to his heart.

"Yes, I see. She will be given much and so much will be required. Then I will constantly pray that humility will be her cloak and that she will rest in You and not deceptive pride." The angel turned his attention back toward his charge and continued to pray for her.

Susan read late into the night and again early the next morning. She had started at the Gospel of John as Paul had suggested and then read the other three Gospels. Next she would start at Genesis and read from the beginning.

She was amazed at how many questions of a lifetime were being answered as she read. She could not understand why she had ever rejected hearing of this book before, and she was thankful that it was now in her possession. She spoke to the Lord as she read, and revelled in the thought that she was now a part of a family and had a Father who loved her. Not only loved her now, but had watched out for her all of her life and had brought her forward to this time when He would reveal himself to her.

I feel so humbled by the fact that You have chosen to show the Ancient path to me. How can I ever thank You enough? I was so lost in my deception, so unaware of all that has been going on around me without my knowledge. Now as I look around me and see how all of the creation speaks of Your glory, how can I ever deny that You exist. How could I have been so blind?

Susan sighed deeply and smiled to herself, hugging the Ancient book to her bosom. *It is a book of love, a promise of hope, isn't it my Lord?*

Adaiah watched Susan intently and listened to her thoughts of the Father. He knew that she would soon be ready to begin her training and he would meet her face to face as he showed her the hidden things that had not yet been revealed.

He thought of when the revelation was given to the Apostle John. John saw the future, but the complete understanding of the revelation has not yet been revealed to the last hour saints. But now Adaiah, along with many other Angels had been given the task of opening the doors of this revelation, and sounding the trumpet to the remnant who had not been contaminated by the Antichrist spirit so at large within the church. Many had been taught that they would simply vanish into thin air one day and the end would come. This was a teaching that had brought idleness to much of the church. Many saints had fallen into a deadly trap as they thought that somehow they had been relieved of bearing the cross of Christ. In fact the teaching of the cross had been lost for so long that the Angel feared for the very life of the Church. He remembered the words of Christ Jesus saying, "Pick up your cross and follow Me," and also, "He who would save his life will lose it, but he who would lose his life for My sake will save his life."

Now it was true that in very few places were there any saints who practised dying to self daily. The angel had often grimaced as he had seen the number of 'the called' who had divorced each other over such things as 'irreconcilable differences.' He knew that a true cross carrying believer would never allow these so called 'differences' to cause a denial of the vows taken to cleave unto a mate 'til death do us part.' That was only one area, there were many other areas where the Called had compromised their faith and joined the world system of belief. One of the worst areas being the neglect of the children, who Christ Himself warned not to be a stumbling block against. The Angel had seen for himself the abuse and neglect of the little ones, as many parents put their own selfish desires above the needs of their children.

He looked again at Bilshan and smiled, he was glad that a new breed of Leaders was about to be revealed to the Church. He looked forward to the day when repentance and reconciliation would bring many of the 'Called' into the status of the 'Chosen.' He thought of the other Angels who were also working on similar assignments, bringing truth and hope to a new generation, even as the children of Israel were finally led out of the wilderness into the promised land. A generation of unbelievers had gone before them, and it had caused much heartache in the camp, and yet when time reached its fulness, a new breed of leaders came forth who were worthy to be called into the promises of God. He smiled to himself as he thought of the future, and the hope that would be birthed. Then he turned again to his charge and closed his eyes and prayed fervently, sending the anointing light from the book she was holding into her heart as she read.

For now Bilshan would be concentrating on learning what was in the Ancient book, soon he would be able to show her what it all meant.

Chapter Nine

At the same time, behind prison walls many miles away, David was also reading with interest the Ancient book. He was stunned to discover that a man named Moses, also a murderer like himself, was chosen to lead the tortured Israelites out of Egypt and into the promised land. Not only that, but Moses was also close to the Living God, and God spoke to him. David was startled within himself as the realization came to him that he too might find this God who did not see as man sees.

Then his hope grew even greater as he read about that other David, who (like himself) had murdered another man out of passion. He saw that this God was different from man, in that He did not withhold His forgiveness for crime when that man saw the folly of his ways.

As David pondered this, he thought of the stain on his life in the form of his prison record, and how it would always be with him no matter where he went, always reminding him of that moment of anger and heartbreak, the loss of his best friend, not to mention the loss of his dear little wife.

How he longed to be forgiven for the mistake, to somehow undo the past and make it right. As he read of this

David of old, he knew of the cry that burst forth from that man's lips, "Create in me a clean heart Oh God!" David cried as he too prayed for a new start in life, a new hope upon which to establish his waking breath each day. He felt weak and vulnerable, yet hope thrust forward in his heart causing him to fall onto his knees and cry out …

"Oh God, if you really exist, please hear my cry, show Yourself to me, free me from the bondage of pain at what I've done. Forgive me for taking another man's life. Give me a new heart, a new life, a new beginning. I have no other hope but in You and this Ancient book of words. Only-let them be more than words if it is possible, let them be life to me, and instill in me a strength to go forward in a new direction." David cried aloud from the depths of his torn heart, not knowing that this cry was the true form of prayer that always brings answers from above.

David's sobs were heard by others in that prison, grown men who wondered at the depth of those sobs, who thought of their own tormented lives, and how they could possibly continue on. They closed their eyes knowingly, and sleep came to shut out the noise of that prison, a place of utter hopelessness.

Little did David know that also there with him in that tiny prison cell was a mighty battle being fought, even as the prayers were being released from his very lips. For the demon strongman named Pinon, meaning Darkness, was angry. He had fought so hard for this soul to be forever lost. When David had murdered his friend, the hideous demon had thought there would be no hope for the man, in fact he had lessened his guard about the man when he had entered the prison because the man was so full of hopelessness.

"How could this have happened?". Pinon raged at the small horde of slimy, suicide demons that he had left in command of the man. "And where did he get that book?", he screamed even louder as he thrashed at the leader of that swarm, causing the demon to revile back with spewing hatred.

"If you are so concerned, then why weren't you here when that angel came and slipped him the book, you idiot," the leader of suicide, nicknamed "Noose" smiled sarcastically.

Just as Pinon was about to undo this little upstart demon, a bright light flashed and a sword of great light and speed came into their midst. Demons were being cut down and obliterated everywhere by the force of this mighty angel who had entered the center of their thicket. The demons fled screaming, and soon the darkness of that cell began to change to a pure light as Putiel, the angel sent to this wayward soul because of the heart prayer that had been prayed, took charge of the atmosphere once belonging to the horde.

As Putiel, who was the very embodiment of his name which meant 'God enlightens,' settled into the room, he smiled and stood close to his unseeing charge, David. As he looked into his eyes, he spoke to David's heart an encouragement saying, *You have been known as Jebus, meaning 'trodden under foot,' but now you shall be Jediael, for you are known by God.* Then the Angel blew his breath over the man, and a light, glittery breeze came forth and settled on David.

He could not see it, but David took in a deep breath of the mist, and as he sighed he somehow felt encouraged as he never had been. It was as if he had been instilled with a faith to believe in this Ancient book and its words, and that he too would be free as both Moses and David of old were free of their sins. David could not help but fall to his face on the floor of his cell as he felt the power of hope flood back into his being. Sobbing loudly, he cried out to the Lord, "Thank you God! I know that You have heard my prayer. Thank you for saving me!"

David spent the entire night on the hard, cold floor of that little cell, too full of wonder and thankfulness to think about it. He cried out a flood of tears in repentance and cleansing for all of his sin and the lifeblood of Jesus flowed freely from the throne of God in answer to the petition of his heart. He repented of his sins, and he believed God, he believed that even though he was beyond hope to many, he was not beyond hope in God. Even Putiel lay on his face next to David, in awe of the great mercy of God that had come to this man.

Putiel was so happy to finally be close to his charge. For many years the Angel had been unable to have close contact with the man due to the demonic company that the man entertained. But the other day, when the evil horde was not aware, the Angel had been able to inconspicuously plant the Ancient book in the prison library, and to bring a light on it that would cause the man to reach for it. Now the man was saved, for he had prayed the prayer of faith that would unleash the blessings of heaven upon him.

The next day, David dove even deeper into the Ancient book, for it seemed to have a new life for him. It was as if it were no longer a dusty old book, but it was a personal message from God for him. It was a handle of heaven, a lifeline to take him away from the hideous life that he had as early as the day before thought was his portion forever.

Putiel looked around the Prison. It was very rare these days for the angels to have entrance into such places. Many Christians feared the prisons and spent very little time trying to lead these lost one's to the Lord of Life, Christ Jesus. Putiel knew that it was all about to change as the revealing of the Remnant drew near. He had seen the vision of the future, that out of these very prisons would come some of the most renown men and women of faith that the world had ever seen. The Lamb of God Himself had already begun to send out the invitations, for many of the people who thought that they were religious enough to get into heaven, had themselves missed the calling of the Lamb. Jesus had told the angels, and the saints who were listening, to go out into the highways and byways, into the prisons and houses of ill repute to send forth the invitation that the marriage supper of the Lamb was about to begin and there were many empty seats yet to be filled.

Chapter Ten

Many months went by as the two students, along with many who are not here mentioned but are also a part of the great Remnant, studied the Ancient book and its teachings. All the angels were kept busy either protecting them, or ministering light and hope to them. As the days passed, the fullness of time was soon upon them and the next phase of training was about to begin.

Once again, Adaiah found himself in a meeting led by Michael the Archangel. Most of the message was an exhortation to be careful about the enemy. The serpent was very deceptive and the elect would need to be very humble in order to fight off the lies that would bombard them. Pride would always be the greatest weapon of Satan, as it was in the beginning. He was the master of pride, and the seed of Adam was very contaminated with it. The Son of God Himself had demonstrated that humility was necessary for survival as He walked the earthly path, it was evident in the recordings of the disciples in the Ancient Book. He was God incarnate, and yet He did not consider equality with God. He found favor in humility, knowing that God resists the proud, the very cause of rebellion of

Satan and one third of all the angels, and yet gives grace to the humble.

The Archangel reminded the angels that grace was the goal for the saints. To be full of grace, even as the Son was, that would be the answer to the horrible seed of Adam that Satan had so contaminated. It was this grace, this empowering presence of God, this fullness, that would enable the saints to be and do all that they were created to do.

As before, all the angels felt renewed in the battle for the Remnant, and they went forth in power.

David had changed so much in the few months since finding the Ancient book that even the guards took notice. Gone was the forlorn quiet man and in his place was this bright, happy, considerate person. He carried a demeanor that seemed to demand the respect of the other inmates and even some of the guards. Whenever he spoke, there was such an air of authority to even the simplest of requests, that it sometimes caused a wondering silence among the other inmates.

David was about to be released on parole, and he was spending several days in fasting and prayer for direction. Since reading the Ancient book, he felt that surely God would show him what he was to do when he was released in the next week. The Holy Spirit was so close to David, especially since he had studied the portion of the Ancient book that taught of the baptism of the Spirit. David had very simply asked that he would be filled, baptized and overcome by the Spirit, and so, because of the prayer of faith, the Spirit was given to him. He thought about the moment of his baptism. He had been in prayer and seeking the Lord for it, yet there was a feeling of desperation. He knew that belief was the necessary ingredient, and yet within him there seemed to be a battle of his will against this belief. He had cried out finally, in uncontrolled passion, "Lord, please help my unbelief!" It was at that moment that the Spirit came, it was as if the ground shook around him, and he fell to the ground in fear. Then a bright light had shown, or something that seemed like light, and he felt shaky, like electricity was surging within his being. After this, as he shook, he laughed and cried at the same time, and then words came. Words that had no earthly meaning, and yet it was as if his very spirit within was somehow connected to the Spirit of God, and he was communicating all the things that had been dammed up within. He let his tongue run free with this new language, and as he did it was as if he were being filled with a new strength and hope. He felt lighter than he ever had in life, and he felt free, more free than he could ever imagine. The sensation was strong and stayed with him for days before he seemed to come down from the mountain top of pleasure that had been his. During this time he was able to witness of his conversion to other inmates, and they would listen to him. It was strange to have a power that was not his own, it was as if he was being worn like a suit by the Lord Himself.

Since David knew nothing of 'religious ways,' He was not weak in his faith, but very strongly bent toward doing the will of the Father in all things. He had lived the past seven years in prison, and yet had found a freedom worth dying for. He even hoped that he would be chosen to give his own life for the Lord of Glory, and return, by that act of love, some of what had been graciously given him in this new life. He longed for Heaven, for the time when he would be with the Father, and his brethren. When the dark veil of the flesh would be lifted and all would be light and life, no more pain, no more tears, and especially for him, no more loneliness.

Putiel was ready to bring more light to David, or Jediael, as he was known to the Angel. The Angel was very big in size, like a giant, and yet he was so gentle and careful with his charge. He would sit with David for hours, touching the Ancient book as the man read, causing certain passages to light up and the man would stop and dwell on them. It was such a pleasure for the Angel to be used to help out the Chosen ones, the Spirit was strong and willing, and the Angel blended himself with the Spirit of God to become the messenger of light and hope. At times his face would be like fire, as the power of the Spirit would come through the Angel to the man, and other times he would resemble a liquid gold that would flow forth and into the heart of the man. That night, while Jediael was asleep, the Angel would come to the man in a dream with the beginning of directions that would bring in a whole new ministry of hope to a lost and dying people.

David awoke early. He wanted to write down the dream that he had just had. He knew in his heart that it was the divine direction that he was looking for. In the dream he had been told to go to a city called 'Madison,' and that off of the main highway there would be a park called 'Riverside Park.' It was known as a haven for the homeless people of the town and he was to go there and wait to meet a woman known as 'SaraJean.' She would be at a drinking fountain on the third day of his stay there and she would listen to him as he told her about the Ancient way.

For the first time in his life he felt as though there was a real meaning to his existence. There was no doubt in him whatsoever that his dream would not come true. His faith was as simple as a little child who might have been told that daddy was going to bring him a treat when he got home. That child would wait at the gate with full expectation because he knew that his daddy never lied, and sure enough when daddy came home, there would be the treat. It was no different for David, he simply knew that he knew that God was going to do what He said.

Chapter Eleven

Susan was with Janna in the kitchen while the others were out in the family room discussing the teaching of that nights meeting. Paul was leading a little study on the Ancient book for her and a few of their neighbors that had shown interest.

Susan smiled as she thought over the past year and the wonderful relationship that she now had with this family. Paul and Janna had all but adopted her, she had spent so much time with them that they had suggested that Susan move in with them and become a part of the family. It did not take Susan long to decide on the move. At about the same time that they had invited her, the rent for her apartment had gone up by $100 making it almost impossible for her to maintain it. She felt that their invitation was from the Father and she was glad to do it.

Living here had been so healing for her. It was as though she had been given these people from the beginning of her life. Janna had become the mother that Susan had never known. In addition Susan had been able to concentrate on learning the Ancient book by not having to work as many hours at her job. Paul had been a great teacher in his own simple way, he lived out the teachings in a practical way that brought a much deeper insight for Susan as she studied.

One of the greatest pleasures for her had been Joy and Katherine. Susan felt like the big sister, and the three of them had become very close. Often they would go to a movie or the mall together and Susan would feel such a blessing in knowing that she was a part of this special family.

"I really love you and Paul and the girls you know." Susan spoke her thoughts aloud to Janna. "I never thought that I would have a family, and I had really given up all hope of it after I had turned 18. Who would have ever thought that God could give me such a family after all." She smiled warmly at Janna.

Janna was just finishing with the snacks that she was putting together. She looked over at Susan and thought of how much she had grown to love this young orphan girl. So much healing had come to her since Susan had been brought into their lives. What with the rejection that they received from their church, it was the best medicine she could have gotten. Susan was one of the Master's own sheep, and the joy at being called to feed one of these dear ones was true ministry, the type of ministry that brought about the joy at being a part of the great heavenly family.

She had seen Susan grow to a point that even now she seemed beyond Paul and herself in understanding. The evident calling upon Susan's life was very encouraging. Last night in bed Paul had commented on it. He was remembering what the Angel had told him about her training.

"He said that she would be trained in the wilderness of the Spirit, and that we should only direct her toward the gospel of salvation, not to teach her any doctrines," was what Paul had said.

It had not been hard to keep her away from Church. Her job had seen to that, for she was usually scheduled to work on Sundays. It did seem strange to Janna that almost every time that Susan had brought up the possibility of attending some Church, thinking that she would be free that day, her schedule at work would suddenly change and she would have to work.

Adaiah was close by as usual. He smiled as he heard what Janna was thinking in regard to Susan, his charge.

Yes, that was right, I went to a lot of trouble to keep her away from those deadly meetings. He thought of those meetings.

The gospel message was preached, but along with it came a deadly poison of works and mans' ways. It was this poison that he must keep away from Bilshan if she was to be able to grow into the faith that she needed to move in. It was sad that so many burdens were put upon the people that they could not just simply believe in what had been done for them. The web of the enemy was so thick that the Angel feared for the life of his charge should she come into contact with it. All reliance upon God was being replaced by trust in man and his own accomplishments. The programs replaced the personal involvement, and many people were falling through the cracks. There were some Churches that were moving according to the Spirit, but they were not anywhere close to this area. Soon that would change as the renewal of the Spirit was coming and the war between the Antichrist and his desire to control the Church would be fought. The Church itself was mostly in a dark age, and many of the saints were having to find their way outside the organized church.

He sighed as he remembered all the homeless people that were aimlessly wandering the streets. If the Church only knew of its true calling to serve, then there would not be near as many of these homeless ones, or the number of suicides, drug overdoses, murders, and the list went on. The Antichrist spirit had taught them that they could hoard for themselves, and call it God's blessings, and that they could live in rich homes having the latest new 'invention,' or eat the best food, and even feed their animals better than some of these street dwellers ate. They were taught that it was okay to have fancy cars, spending more money on some of them than the poor lived on in a whole year. What had happened to the early Church, when they had all things in common? When a man had more money, he did not keep it, but he gave it to those around him so that they all had equal. Not only that, but the Elders had the wisdom that is from above and knew how to disperse the money fairly, the result being that everyone had plenty, and also extra to share with others. The widows and fatherless were also cared for by the Church, and there was no need for something like 'food stamps' in their midst.

Now things were changing, in fact it was right at the doorstep. The hopeful Angel stopped and looked longingly at his charge. Bilshan would be a part of a new era. She was part of the remnant. He was ready to begin showing her the ways of the Spirit.

That next day, Susan was very upset as she came home from work. She had come in through the kitchen door and headed straight for her room. The look on her face told Janna that there was a problem. Janna followed her into her bedroom and asked if everything was okay.

"I was laid off from my job today," Susan sighed as she spoke. "It was so odd. I really don't understand it. They called me into the office, and the manager said that they had hired too many last month, and although my work was of good quality, they needed to let me go. When I asked him 'why me', he said that they had chosen by lottery whom they would lay off, and my name was picked."

Susan had a perplexed look upon her face. "Don't you think it strange that they didn't let go of one of the more recent hires, instead of me? I've been there for more than two years. Janna, I just don't get it, why me?" She looked at Janna imploringly.

Even as Susan was speaking, Janna felt the quickening of the Holy Spirit within her saying that this was of God, and that she should encourage Susan to trust in His plan for her life. Janna reached out for Susan and drew her into a big, healthy hug.

"Don't worry sweetheart, God is in control. Remember the teaching from the Ancient book that says, 'He will never leave you or forsake you'. Susan you must put this into His hands and tell Him that you trust in His plan for your life. " Janna continued to hold Susan as she spoke.

Susan felt herself relax into Janna's motherly arms. Oh how comforting it was to have someone to hold and cherish her. She let herself linger in the hug, as if drinking in the embrace for every time in her lost youth when there were no such hugs available. She listened to the soft words of trust that Janna spoke and tried to let go of her anxieties. After a few long moments, she stepped back from the embrace and looked at Janna.

"Thanks Janna, I really needed that. And of course your right, I know that I need to trust Him. I do have a little saved up, I was thinking of taking some college courses, but I can use the money to live on for a while if needed." Susan smiled meekly as she spoke, she was trying to put her trust in the Lord as she spoke. She felt as if the rug had been pulled out from under her.

Janna smiled her motherly smile. "Don't worry about your living expenses here. You can eat with us and live here as long as you want to. We have plenty to include you also. Besides, you're just like one of my own daughters. We really love having you here." Janna spoke sincerely. She reached out and brushed the soft brown hair away from Susan's eyes, letting her hand linger on her head as she looked into the young woman's hazel eyes. "You are so special. You know that?"

How could she convey in words how much Susan meant to her? She silently prayed the Father would show Susan that she really was a part of this family. She had often prayed the girl would be healed of the hard years that she had endured as an orphan, for she knew in her heart God was able to restore all that had been stolen from this dear, young friend.

Later that night when Paul came home, Janna told him about the conversation that she had with Susan and how the Lord had reassured her that this was in His plan. Paul listened intently and prayed as she spoke.

"Susan is about to begin the training that I was told about." Paul sighed and looked upward. "It's funny though, I really don't know what to expect. I wish I knew how the Father is going to prepare her. I haven't seen the angel since that day at the hospital. I thought that I would see him more often by the way he sounded, but all has been silence. Even my prayer time has been quiet, almost boring, and I've really had to pray by faith. But by this I know something is up." Paul took a deep breath and continued.

"Janna, get ready for a change, somehow I feel that it is time for Susan's training to begin." Paul spoke with a sense of wonder. He had questioned the things that had happened recently because of the season of quiet that was upon him spiritually. Now that things were changing, he felt the stirring of the Spirit within him.

"Don't wait up for me tonight, I have a feeling that its going to be a long night," he spoke almost absently as he walked out of the bedroom. It was time to pray, and he felt very expectant.

Chapter Twelve

David stopped and looked back at the prison. He had just been released on parole, and he was standing outside the tall iron gates looking at the place where he had spent the longest period of his life at one time. The buildings were huge, with dark grey stone and tall, barbed wire fences surrounding them. The land around the prison was desolate and barren. The sky that day was as grey as the walls. A lone black bird cawed as he flew out across the open yard where David once walked for exercise. The bird's cry reminded David of the pain that was part of the place, desolation, darkness, loneliness and fear.

He was both thankful and sad for his experience. He would always regret the action that brought him here, the murder of his friend. But he was grateful for the new life that he found in the Savior. As he looked at the prison, he recounted all these things and spoke out loud to the Lord of his life.

"From this day forward, everything that I do is for you. My life I will live only to see that day when I will behold You, the One who saved me from a sure, eternal death," he spoke the words with tears and heartfelt love. He now belonged to another country, an unseen country, for his home was eternal, and now his life was to be given in the same way that his Lord had given His dear life, for the lost, all for the lost.

As he boarded the bus that was to take him to the nearest town, he spoke to the bus driver. "How far is it to Madison, sir?" David inquired.

"It's about three hours south of here. But you might have trouble getting there today, the bus runs there once a day and that was at seven a.m. I'm going to the main depot now over in Henderson," the driver spoke roughly. He was an old man with deep wrinkles in his forehead, as though he had worried over every day of his life.

"That's fine. I'll head into town for now. Thanks," David smiled at the man, and it caused the man to wonder since smiles were something that rarely came his way. David boarded toward the back of the bus. As he sat down, he looked into the envelope that the prison had discharged him with to see how much cash he was allowed. "Fifty dollars won't last long," he thought to himself. "I may just try to hitchhike instead of taking a bus," he thought as he made his plans.

The bus ride from the prison to the town was about an hour, and David prayed all the way. He felt so different, being released from his planned out life, and into this big open space. It was a big change for him. He could relate, just for a moment with those repeat offenders' who seemed bent on being sent back to prison as soon as they were released. Prison held a sort of perverted security, it was a place to belong to, a place that had a law all it's own and a hierarchy of rank and authority among the inmate's. He had watched as men laughed at the inmate's who were being released shouting, "You'll be back, you can't live without us and you know it!" And so often they were right. Even though most inmates' shouted right back that they would never return, the majority of them often came back. They even returned with a swagger as if to say it was the plan all along.

As the bus sped along the deserted highway, he could see how easy it could happen, especially to men who did not have any other hope in life. David smiled knowing that his hope was in the Truth, the Living Truth who had Himself come to earth as a man and showed the way to eternal life. Jesus Christ, this Truth and Son of the Living God, had won the victory for all mankind. Any who would accept His death in their own place and receive His life instead of what they deserved could live in the same hope that David had received. The simplicity of the gospel of Christ was almost hard to believe. He knew that many had tried to complicate it, to somehow put a price on what had been so freely given.

He saw it in the Ancient book. People who lived in a place called Galatia had fallen prey to the influence of works. How could anyone in their right mind think that they could do anything or enough to earn a place in heaven. Besides, if it were possible to find some other way to eternal life, why would the creator of the Universe so painfully clothe Himself in the frailty of the flesh in vain, and suffer the horrible death of the cross for nothing?

Putiel, David's angel, was there with him administering light as David thought. The angel was planning how he would be the one who picked up David when he tried to hitch a ride. The captain of his fighting angel's had warned him that the enemy was about, and it probably wasn't safe for David to hitchhike.

The angel had only appeared to man one time before this, and he thought of it now. It was when David's great-grandfather was a young man. He was a wayward soul at the time, and the enemy was about to steal his life from him. The man was getting ready to board a train that was sabotaged by the enemy and the angel had appeared as a lost child who needed help. David's great-grandfather had just missed the train while taking the lost child to the station office. The train wrecked and many lives were lost, but not that man, nor this one, his great-grandson. God's plan for David had begun many years earlier, but this knowledge would have to wait til the great day of revelation, when all would be revealed in heaven and earth.

And now he was to be an angel dressed in man's clothing.

David was soon at the little town that was closest to the isolated prison. He walked about trying to take in all the changes that had occurred since he had been incarcerated. He stopped at a small department store that was displaying televisions in the front window. The TV's were blaring out a show that caused David to blush at its content. He was wondering to himself how this could be on a daytime show, the language that was being used, and the sexual innuendo's, what was going on? He had not watched TV much during the time that he was in prison, mainly due to the fact that the TV room was not a safe place to be. In his quest for personal safety, he had become out of touch with what was happening in the world. Now as he watched, he wondered if other people still watched. Surely it was not popular if this was what was being shown. Maybe this was the only show of this type and it wasn't all this bad. Just as he was thinking of these things, a commercial came on the air. He had to cover his eyes as a woman was shown in her underwear. He quickly glanced around to see if anyone was looking, for he felt shamed as if he was participating in some hidden sin. But as he looked around, he saw that no one even noticed or looked, it was as though this was somehow acceptable. He caught his breath as he saw a young child of about eight or nine pass by and look nonchalantly at the partially clad woman as if it was common to view such things.

He felt shaken to the bone. A chill went through him. How could the world have changed so much? He tried to remember how TV was before he went into the prison, but he couldn't remember it being anything like what he had just seen. He walked away, shaking his head in confusion. As he walked, he started to look around him with different eyes. How were people different now? He knew that immorality had been a problem since the 60's, that was what had gotten him into so much trouble in the first place. His wife supposedly had 'every right' to sleep with whomever she wanted to, even though she was married to David. But it had not always been that way. America had taken a dive into the cesspool of immorality and idolatry from what he could see. Even this small town had not escaped the evil influence that had covered the land like a thick spider web, sticking itself to every moving object and engulfing it in the tomb of webbing.

He saw the run down town through different eyes as he beheld the closed up shops', the vandalism to the area, spray painted graffiti on the walls, broken windows, trash in the streets, young people lazing about on the street corners with cigarettes hanging from their lips, an empty look in their eyes. The sounds of sarcasm weaving wickedly throughout the whole scene as if some malignant cancer was growing rapidly in their midst, swallowing up every 'clean' cell and leaving a deformed, useless mess in its place.

Even the little church on the corner of one street had not escaped the path of destruction. It was broken down, over-grown weeds in the front, trash strewn about, and a message on the little paint peeled billboard proclaiming "God Loves Y-u," minus a letter. There was nothing attractive about this little building that said what God had to offer was any different from anything else around this town.

As he was walking through the town, and thinking these thoughts silently to himself, he was not paying attention to a group of young people directly ahead of him in his path, until he suddenly found himself in their midst.

"Hey man, what are you doing on my @$#% sidewalk?", a young man of about 12 or 13 cursed at David. As the boy cursed, he pulled out a sharp knife and pointed it in David's face.

David stopped and stared at the young man who was not quite tall enough to reach David's shoulders, but had a look on his face that matched some of the most fearsome criminals with whom he had recently been incarcerated.

"I did not know that this sidewalk belonged to you," he lamely replied, being taken off guard by this whole situation, and feeling utterly shocked by the words and expression of this mere youth. He wanted to run away, but was unsure of how to respond to such a threat by one so young. He could see the friends of this young man begin to tighten the circle around him and he knew that he needed to act fast or he could get hurt.

The angel was there, waiting and watching, allowing David to see and experience the evil that was loose in the town. It was a needed lesson for the man, planned to teach him what he would need to know. Now it was time for the rescue. The angel swiftly flew around a corner and appeared as a man driving a late model truck. He drove out of an alley and came up to the curb just as the circle was about to close in on David.

"Quick! Jump in the truck," he yelled to David as he pulled up in front of the scene. The angel resembled an elderly farmer.

David saw the opening and dove for the truck just as the youngster took a swipe with his knife and missed. Somehow David felt himself being lifted up and put into the truck as if by unseen hands.

Putiel, the angel, thanked his ever present army of fighting angels' for the boost to the man, and hit the gas.

David took a breath of air and filled his starving lungs, he had forgotten to breathe in the midst of the fast-moving action that almost cost him his life. He turned to the farmer, "Thanks man, you just saved my life."

The 'farmer' smiled at David, and a little light escaped his eyes causing David to relax into the peace of the atmosphere created by the angel's presence.

"That's okay son. I'm just glad I came up when I did or you might have a few holes in you right about now." The farmer spoke softly to the man.

David felt as if he had gone from excessive evil into the extreme opposite of goodness, he could not quite put his finger on the feeling he felt around the farmer, but it was something like what he had felt around his father as a child. Strangely secure was as close as he could come. David turned and looked out the window of the truck. He saw the young man waving his hand in the air making an obscene gesture. His mouth was moving in what David was sure were obscenities. David felt a chill as he looked back at the evil scene. He looked at the serene farmer in wonder. Since he could think of nothing else to say he turned to the farmer and sought information.

"So where are you headed?" David spoke shakily.

"I'm on my way out to Madison to pick up some feed. Where can I drop you, son?" came the gentle reply.

"You're headed for Madison? Wow. That's great. Can I ride along with you? I need to get to Madison myself." David spoke hurriedly, not believing his luck and the miracle he had just witnessed.

"Sure son, I'd love to have the company," the farmer encouraged David, "So where you from? What's your name? Tell me your story son." The farmer looked at David inviting him to share his story and enjoy the ride.

Chapter Thirteen

Paul had just begun to settle into his prayer time when he felt the atmosphere of the room change. He looked around the room. Everything was in its place. The soft pastel hues of the decor began to vibrate with an almost electric presence. The couch, the big soft recliner that he often found himself relaxing in after a hard days work, even the small chairs that he had made for his two daughters to sit in while they watched TV; the whole room slowly changed as he watched. It was as if every cell of each item were pulsing with life, how else could one explain the presence of the supernatural among the natural?

His skin felt like a solid goose bump, and he felt a fear rise up in his flesh as the light of the room took on an unearthly glow. Then he began to see a celestial figure appear in the center of the room. Down to his face on the carpet he went. He could not help himself. It was a natural inclination of the flesh to respond to something holy by bowing down. Next he heard Susan's angel, Adaiah, speak.

"Anaiah, the girl you know as Susan is about to be brought into the wilderness of the Spirit. She will be unreachable in her earthly vessel for many days. You are not to be concerned, for she will be okay. Have your wife attend to her physical needs as she is in this sleeping state, and whenever she speaks, record the words that she is saying. Do not try to wake her up, for she will not awaken until the time is ready for her earthly journey to resume."

The angelic being looked at Paul and smiled, this man was so willing to serve. He could see the man trembling and fighting himself to remain calm and sure, as if it were a common experience to entertain angels face to face. Adaiah felt himself wanting to give the man more encouragement for his own ministry. The Spirit was there and ready for this to happen, so Adaiah reached out to Paul and touched him. The man nearly fainted as the angel touched him, but the angel looked deep into his eyes and brought a calming effect to Paul's jittery nervous system.

Taralah, Paul's angel then appeared. He stood next to Adaiah and smiled warmly at Paul. Adaiah spoke, "Anaiah, this is your guardian Angel, Taralah." Adaiah turned toward the other angel and gestured. "He will be close to you and help you as you serve the Most High God. You have been given a gift of power to heal as you go forward and give the message of the gospel of salvation. The gospel is the power of God to transform lives. Be confident, and have faith that as you go, the Spirit will be with you and guide you. The time for the return of the Son is close at hand. You will be an Elder to many of the young ones who have been chosen to usher in the end of the age. These 'young ones' are the little children even now being birthed, and you will be to them as Joshua was to the generation of children born in the wilderness during the Exodus, as it is written in the Ancient book. That is why Susan is being taught by the Spirit in the wilderness, she will also be a leader and teacher of the young one's. Her training will be on a different level than what you know of. She is of their generation and will be a mighty warrior of purpose." Adaiah stopped and gazed into

Paul's eyes to be sure that he understood all that was being said. Paul was standing, still trembling a bit, but much calmer than before. As the angel spoke, his heart quickened. He had felt that this younger generation were to be the one's who would usher in the end of the age, but now he was hearing it spoken by an angel. So that was the plan. Well it all made sense to him. These little one's were the offspring of the children of the 70's. But these had not been subject to the teaching of the Antichrist since many of the people born in the 70's had rejected the church. This was the 90's and these young parents were now called 'generation X'. Many of them had participated in having abortion's so he knew that some of the 'little one's' had been stolen away. One thing that had stood out to him though, was the fact that these children were being raised in a time when magic and fantasy was everywhere in front of them. He thought of the popular cartoons that his children watched and how often he saw prophetic parallels in them. Maybe God was bringing these little one's into an arena of faith without the enemy knowing or suspecting it.

As Paul was thinking these thoughts, the angel spoke to him that he was right in his suspicions.

Then Taralah spoke to Paul, "We have been waiting for these little one's to be birthed. When you read the Ancient book, you can see that there is a generation of people who will not be compromised to the ways of the Antichrist spirit. They will be warriors, arrows in the hands of the Elders who will guide them into the last battle where the Saints will overcome the evil one. Then the Son will come on a White Horse and these warriors' will be at the forefront of the final battle, followed by all the Saints who are even now preparing for the final engagement between light and darkness. The Antichrist spirit has lulled many of the called into believing that they will be taken out of the earth or defeated by the enemy. They have put their hope into being transported away somehow. The young one's will not receive this. They will fight for the Truth, and they will give their lives for the truth. Then all the 'Martyr Thrones' in heaven will be filled by them. Because they will fight even to the loss of their own lives, then they will gain eternal life even more abundantly. This is the true 'defeat' of the enemy, that the flesh is overcome by the Spirit. They will never give up the fight, even to their dying breath they will proclaim "Salvation belongs to our God who sits on the throne, and to the Lamb!"

The room grew brighter with each word as the angel spoke and something Holy began to fill the air as a blue smoke infiltrated the atmosphere. The angels themselves began to bow low as the Son Himself appeared to Paul. Jesus Christ appeared, clothed in a white radiant garment, His eyes like a flame of fire, His hand's nail scarred. He stood tall and stately, looking at Paul with compassion and love, reaching His hands out toward one for whom He gave His life.

"I Am coming soon! Tell them Anaiah! Warn them of the hour! The time is near for the completion of all things and you must be ready." Pure divinity spoke aloud. As He spoke the room vibrated with the sound of a thundering river, as though His voice were made of all the sounds ever created.

Paul was on the floor along with the angels, bowing low in reverence to the One who had all the keys of life and death in His hands. Paul's thoughts were riveted upon this One who had overcome the wickedness of the world and offered life to any who would simply turn to Him and receive His blood sacrifice in place of their own sin. Paul saw for himself, as he lay prostrate and his vision was expanded, just how wonderful the message of the gospel really was, and how simple. He thought to himself, *If only*

I could preach the simplicity of this gospel, the true love that rests at its core, no doctrine, no condemnation, but simple and pure Love. It really would change the world. With compassion that would melt the heart of the hardest criminal, Jesus put His hand out toward Paul and lifted him up to his feet. "Do not fear my son, I AM and I will be with you in all these ways. Do not concern yourself with those who have made a law out of My grace. The invitation has gone forth and My Father has called for a great feast to be held in My honor. It is for My coming marriage, and the banquet hall is not yet filled. I have not come for those who are well, but for the sick. Go to those who are sick, the ones who need Me and My lifeblood. I will give you words and My Spirit will be with you as He was with Me on My earthly journey. I came as a servant, and you must also serve. Lay down your life, for those who try to preserve themselves, trying to serve two masters, will not be a part of my Kingdom. You cannot have two accounts, you either have your account here on the earth, where rust and moth and decay will set in and steal, or have your treasure stored up in My Kingdom, where it multiplies for all eternity in ways that you cannot even comprehend. Live simple lives, just as I showed you in the Ancient book. I have called you to give to the poor, yet I see many who would call them-selves your brethren who have taken the money intended to feed the poor and train up those called to preach My words, and they have padded themselves in luxury. Many have become as those Pharisee's who walked about piously while their hearts were deep holes full of maggots, feeding off the wounds of the needy. Do not let these men who want to control and abuse My sheep cause you to fear. They use My teachings in ways that I did not intend, just as those Pharisee's did, to build up their own ego and to have a following of people who will worship them. My Kingdom is not of such as these, it is rather given to those who share their cloak when they see their neighbor in need, and who concern themselves with those who are suffering in prisons of shame and condemnation. I have called you to the task of preaching My message of truth, that I have come to set the captive free, releasing them from their prison of sin and training them to share the message to all who will hear."

At this point the Son sighed deeply and tears filled His eyes. He looked at Paul with a look that caused Paul to gasp for breath and cry out. "Oh Lord, what is it? What has caused you so much pain?" Paul wanted to tear his clothes apart to see such agony on the face of his dear Savior.

Jesus looked up toward heaven for a moment and drew His breath in slowly. "Anaiah, so many have been left in pain and suffering and their cries reach the heavens each minute of the day. It should not be so." He sighed deeply again, as if the pain that was caused by these cries was piercing His very heart. "When I look at My people who have been called by My Name, and I see many of them, day after day, sitting and listening to men preach a worn out message over and over again, it grieves Me. I never intended for so many to sit and do nothing, and it has caused a great void in the salvation of the lost. I called for My followers to preach the gospel and to make disciples of those who are saved. To do this would mean that more and more disciples would be out preaching and doing the works of the gospel. When the gifts I have given are not taught and encouraged to operate, then the plan of salvation is not preached in its fullness. Here is an example of what should be done, when you lead a lost one into the truth of salvation, begin at once to also train them to participate in the work even as they are being healed and set free. Many men and women who are called to be 'Pastors' do not understand the truth of their calling. To be a shepherd does not imply ownership, but rather provision for food and growth, and release to calling. I have called some to be pastors, some teachers, some evangelists, some prophets, and some apostles. To each there is a place to serve. The service that I speak of is not in buildings but in people. When the remnant goes forth in the truth that was given to the early church as written in the book of Acts, they will once again have all things in common and salvation of the lost will be the primary focus of each body of believers. Because of the fruit of the Spirit, given as you come and have a personal and intimate relationship with Me, you will have the love that is necessary to do My Father's will. The fullness of the gifts will be in operation and you will not find people languishing in the pews. In fact, the men and women who now spend so much time 'in front', will be found in 'back' busily washing the feet of new converts as I have called them to do."

The Master looked tenderly at Paul. "I know that you have suffered much rejection, but it is necessary for the pain to work in you a stronger desire not to do what has been done to you. I allow pain to be a guide and companion so that you do not walk after the ways of the flesh. Anaiah, I want you to go out and find the sick, the demonized, those who are in prisons of addiction and fear. Go to them and I will give you words of encouragement for them, you will bring them to Me and I will heal them through you. These angels will help you even as they helped Me during My earthly walk. I love you!" As Jesus spoke these last words, He began to ascend upward through the ceiling of the room, as though His presence were only an apparition. He was lost to the visual sight of Paul, yet His words remained as a piercing sword in his heart.

"Yes my Lord, I will go and serve You. I will go as You have asked. I love You Lord!" Paul replied with tears of joy.

Chapter Fourteen

Meanwhile, Susan was lying awake in her bed. She tossed and turned for a moment. Then she sat up and looked around the room. It was a dark night, and yet there was a light that seemed to be without origin. All around the room this light began to penetrate. She looked at the soft quilt on her bed, the beautiful rose pattern in the center of the blanket even glowed. She felt the quickening of the Spirit within her heart. She tried to pray, but felt strangely intimidated by her awareness of another presence in the room. "Who's there?" she called out into the space around her, hearing her own voice echo back unanswered.

Just as suddenly she found herself in another place, as if she were translated without knowledge of how she got there. It was a strange place, like a desert. It was hot, and dry, with sand dunes and stark hills surrounding her. She felt loneliness engulf her being, a type of loneliness that she had never before experienced in her life.

"Hello! Is anyone out there?" She called out into the dry, gentle breeze. But only the soft whisper of the wind answered her. *What is going on here? I must be dreaming.* She thought to herself. She pinched herself hard, crying out 'ouch' from the pain of it. *I wonder if you can pinch yourself in a dream and feel a response as part of the dream,* she thought to herself again. *Oh well, if this is a dream, then I guess I will start walking and see where I end up.* She started walking toward some distant hills, looking for any sign of life as she went.

After walking for what seemed to be hours, she finally came upon a young man sitting alone on a rock. She tried to talk to him, but for some strange reason he was not aware of her presence, it was as if she were invisible to him. She got very close to him and tried to touch him, but her hand was somehow transparent and went right through him. She tried again, slowly. She put out her hand to touch the young man, again nothing. It was as if she were caught in another realm, somewhere between the living and the dead.

Am I dead or something? She thought to herself, feeling fear well up inside of her. But even as the fear came, there was also a sense of peace and she felt the presence of the Spirit.

Susan, watch and learn. I am with you always. The still small voice of the Spirit spoke into her heart. She closed her eyes and let the calming peace of the Spirit soothe over her. Then slowly she opened her eyes and with those comforting words and the peace that she felt, she relaxed, walked over to a rock and sat down, then watched the young man.

Now here is a strange looking character, she thought. The young man was sitting on a rock, looking out toward a river about a 1/4 mile from where he was sitting. She looked toward the river and could see that it was green and pretty in comparison to the stark nakedness of the terrain over which she had just journeyed. The young man himself was dressed in some sort of animal skin. It was a thick leathery black hide. He was rugged looking as if he had spent most of his life out in the dry wind of this desert. His skin was dark brown and he had a full head of wild black hair that went in every direction just like the endless sand dunes surrounding them. He seemed to be sitting with a sense of anticipation, as though waiting for a signal or something. Then she heard a soft rustle of something close by, and she watched as the man reached around the rock he was sitting on and spoke to a little lamb that was sitting in the shade, previously hidden from her view.

The man spoke softly to the little animal, caressing it gently. She could not understand the words that he used, he spoke in a language that she did not understand, but she could see that the little lamb was precious to the man. It reminded her of a little stray kitten that she had found when she was a little girl. The way he caressed the lamb and spoke soft sweet words to it, what a nice feeling she got from watching them.

Then, from the direction of the river, a voice called out to the young man. Susan looked and saw a man waving his hand at the young man and yelling something. The man who called was also dressed in strange attire, like ancient clothing belonging to a different time. He was wearing layers of cloth, like a dress almost, it reminded her of a movie she had seen once about the time when Jesus walked on the earth. She watched as the young man got up and took the little young lamb in his arms and walked toward the man who had waved at him. She followed.

As they came closer to the man, she saw that he had piled a bunch of rocks and made what looked like a crude table or something. On top of it was a pile of wood, branches and twigs, set neatly as if waiting to be lit for a nice little camp fire. The man gestured toward the young man and his lamb, and showed him a knife like object, a stone that had been shaped and sharpened.

The young man looked at the older man, tears welling up in his eyes as if pleading with him. The older man nodded his head in sorrow and gestured toward the stone table.

Then Susan watched in horror as the young man took the little, helpless lamb and tied him up with a rope that the older man gave him. As he gently secured the little lamb, his tears fell freely on the animals' head and he wept openly. The older man handed him the stone-knife, as the young man held the lamb tightly and kissed its head.

Susan knew what was about to happen and started to protest loudly, charging toward the young man and his lamb, when suddenly she felt her arm being grabbed by someone. She gasped and looked to see who was there, turning she was startled to see what she immediately perceived to be an angel.

"Who are you?" Susan cried out, shocked at his presence.

"I am Adaiah. I am your guardian angel." Adaiah smiled softly. "I am here to guide you through the wilderness of the Spirit. You must watch and learn from what you are about to see." The angel spoke gently to Susan.

Just as Susan was about to question the angel further, the young man took the lamb and walked over to the table with the firewood on it.

"You have to stop him. He is going to kill the little lamb." She cried out to the angel, pleading with him to do something.

The angel held her arm firmly and spoke quietly, sadness emanating from his eyes, "This is necessary for you to see, little one. You must feel the pain and know the truth of these things." Gently he turned Susan toward the scene and held her still.

Then the young man cried out in a loud voice, as if calling to the heavens, and he put the little lamb on the wood. He seemed to be petitioning God for a way out of the horrible thing that he was about to do. The older man sat and watched with tears also falling freely down the deep creases of his age worn face. The young man took the little lamb in his arms again in one last heart rendering embrace, then setting it on the wood again, he held it down as he took the knife and cut the throat deeply.

Chapter Fifteen

The blood spurted out from the mortal wound on the little lamb's throat, as a meek little bleat of protest escaped its dying muzzle. The blood filtered down over the wood and made a little pool on the center of the table. The young man set about sparking a fire to consume the sacrifice that he had just made.

Susan sat down quietly upon a nearby rock. "Why did he do it?" she spoke in almost a whisper to the angel standing beside her.

The angel looked carefully at his charge, feeling the pain he knew she felt upon the death of the little lamb. "It was necessary for the atonement of sin before the Lamb of God became the final sacrifice for all sin." He spoke with deep compassion, his voice breaking as the tears began to stream from his face. "The young man that you see is known as John the Baptist, and the older man is his father, the priest Zacharias. John is being taught by his father of the ways of the covenant. The cry that you heard from John was that the true Lamb of God would come and give the final atonement. His tears over the little pet lamb were more for the cost that would be paid by the Son, than for his own loss of his little lamb, though he had loved that little lamb for quite some time."

"The heart of John was trained here, in the desert. He was raised up to herald in the coming of the Savior in the flesh, who even now in John's time, is alive. As you have read in the Ancient book, John will baptize his cousin, the one known as Jesus of Nazareth." The angel watched as Susan listened to his words. "You are also called to herald the coming of the Savior. For it is time for the second coming of the Lamb of God, this time not as a Lamb, but as a Lion. He will return and destroy His enemies, and His chosen one's will be right by His side. First His bride must make herself pure, and there are many who have not yet come into the Light of His truth. Just as John cried out for repentance, you also must cry out and warn of the return of the Lion of the tribe of Judah. There is a great harvest of lost soul's who are yet to hear and receive new life. You must understand the truth of the gospel before you can proclaim it. That is why you have been brought here." His eyes showed a tenderness and love as he spoke, Susan immediately warmed to this unusual presence, noting that he was very tall, at least seven feet or more, and also that he seemed to have a liquid gold hair. She had never seen an angel before, and for the moment it mesmerized her to think that she was now in the presence of one.

As Susan watched and listened to the angel, she had many deep thoughts. *Why is it that I am not shocked by his presence? This whole place, this scene before me seems so unreal. Yet I know what his is saying is true.* She sighed. She felt very overwhelmed by such a calling on her life, and knew that she did not have the type of commitment necessary for such a ministry.

"How can this happen to me? I am just a girl, a simple-minded girl. Surely you have the wrong person. There are so many more anointed people than me. What about Paul or

Janna? They are much closer to the Lord than I." Susan looked helplessly at the angel.

"Paul and Janna also have their callings and will be used. There are many who are a part of the remnant and will usher in the last battle. Do not fear, little one, you are a vessel chosen for the work of the Spirit. You are known in the heavens as 'Bilshan'. You are created to be a seeker of the truth. It is the Spirit who gives ability. You must only be available to be used. First you must understand the gospel and what it really is about. Follow John as he fulfills his destiny. Learn from him." The angel gestured toward the young man who now stood alone watching the final wisp of smoke ascend into the heavens from the ashes of the dear little lamb that was no more.

Susan watched the young man, and saw herself in him as he searched the skies for the answer to his cries.

Then as suddenly as she had appeared in this place, she found herself in another place, similar but different. She was still standing by the river, but now the young man was full grown and there was a crowd of people gathered around him as he spoke loudly to them. John was large and thick in his stature, with hair more wild than before and piercing blue eyes that seemed to see beyond whatever they focused on. His arms were big and hairy, and he wore an animal skin similar to the one he wore as a youth. His voice echoed easily through the crowd as if amplified supernaturally. When he spoke there was such a stillness among the people as they hung on every word this strange man spoke. She could see that the people feared him, yet respected him carefully. John himself was strangely removed from the common, as if he knew his destiny was as the Baptist, and there was no other thought in his life.

Though she still could not understand the words spoken, it seemed that she learned even more from the gestures and surroundings of what was happening. John was reaching out his hands to help a small crippled boy who had come to be baptized. The boy looked very sick and sad, his mother was with them as John gently picked up the boy and took him out to the water. As John held the boy, tears streamed down his face as he looked up toward the heavens and cried out loud. His cry seemed to plead for the little boy to be healed, it was a cry of help. John lifted the boy toward the heavens then descended him into the water, for the rite of baptism to be completed. Then he walked back slowly through the water, bracing himself against the current and returned the little child to the arms of his mother.

Even as this was occurring, a group of men clad in priestly garments stood at the shore side with looks of disgust on their faces. She watched them as they whispered among themselves and pointed at the throng gathered at the water's edge. As she followed their pointing fingers, she saw what they were looking at. Off a short way from the crowd gathered another group of people, different from the rest of the crowd in that they were covered with bloody bandages, and old rags. She saw that they were regarded as outcasts and many of the people feared them as though they carried a plague of some sort.

"Who are those people?" Susan questioned the angel who stood quietly at her side.

"They are known as Lepers because they carry a contagious disease on their outward flesh." The angel sadly looked into Bilshan's eyes. "It is the same with the human soul, Bilshan. If all these people who are keeping their distance from these 'outcasts' could see the condition of their own soul, they would shudder at the sight of it. But most do not see the truth of their own condition. Those priests over there are even worse, for they do not bleed within anymore, they have lost all compassion for the suffering and their souls resemble open graves. John is able to see as you are now seeing. The condition of all mankind is in likeness to those lepers. Rottenness consumes all and there is no cure for it. Sin has separated all who exist on this planet, this creation of the triune God."

"Do you remember reading in the Sacred text, the story of the beginning of all time?" The angel inquired of the girl.

"Yes, I've read the story of Adam and Eve, and how they chose rebellion by eating of the fruit of the wrong tree." Susan responded eagerly, craving understanding of what she was seeing in front of her.

"Yes, that's right," replied the angel, smiling at Susan encouragingly. "I can see that you have learned as you have studied! When God spoke of death coming to the man and woman if they partook of the fruit of the forbidden tree, that was the beginning of this disease that consumes all souls. It is the death that was spoken of. They died that day, the moment when the fruit was consumed. It was a spiritual death which brought a great chasm of darkness between the Creator and all of His creation. God is Light and cannot abide with darkness, man allowed darkness to be birthed into his soul at that moment. You must see that there is no hope in the arm of the flesh. Come with John as he ministers to the lepers. As you watch, remember that all is as hopeless for the human soul as what you are seeing in the flesh of these lepers. Know that this disease is an outward manifestation of the internal condition of all mankind." The angel gently touched Susan's arm as he guided her toward the man John.

John also saw the priest's and their pointing fingers. He looked at them with a look of severe reproving as he spoke to them and pointed his finger in their faces. She could not understand the words, but she knew what they meant. John then started to walk toward the lepers. Susan saw the crowd gasp and cry out in warning him not to go any closer. John continued boldly ahead with a look of deep compassion on his face. Then the lepers themselves began to shout and wave their arms toward John as if warning him not to come any closer. He did not stop. Still closer he came, until he stood with arms outstretched in front of one of the leprous men.

Susan watched with tears streaming down her face. She felt her heart squeeze tight as she sighed out loud. "He really loves them, doesn't he?" she spoke absently to the angel. Adaiah only nodded in agreement as he too watched this display of love in awe.

Then they looked on as John took the sick man in his arms and walked with him toward the water. He gently removed the layers of bandage and exposed the wretched wounds. The crowd gasped and many turned away at this point as John kissed the man on his cheek. Blood and skin, infected and weeping on the man's face, mixing with tears as the man wept over the encounter of true love that he was experiencing. John, himself weeping, took the man and began to wash his many wounds in the water of the river. Looking up toward the heavens, he called out to God for mercy.

"You have also been as one of these leprous ones, Bilshan. All are lost without the salvation wrought by Christ. John is able to go to them because he is not deceived into thinking that he is any different from them, he knows of the true condition of the soul, that all is hopeless with man. Unless a great salvation comes from heaven, there is no hope. Even though you have received this salvation through your acceptance of Jesus, you must understand that you can never offer hope, or give assistance to any who are lost without knowing Jesus Christ is the only source of hope."

"It is very easy for the Antichrist spirit to deceive you into thinking that you somehow deserve to be saved, or that you have earned the grace that has been so freely given. Until you know in your heart that all glory and honor belong to Him, the Savior, and Him only, then you cannot be entrusted with power. For this to happen, you must see with unveiled eyes the true condition of your soul without Him. Never forget what you are seeing, child, never forget!" The angel spoke with piercing intensity while looking into Susan's eyes.

Susan turned from the angel at this point and again watched as John helped the pitiful leper back to the shore.

Chapter Sixteen

David enjoyed the ride with the old farmer, even though the man had very little to say. He had a way of pulling David's life story out of him, but to David's surprise it felt very good sharing about his imprisonment and newly found faith. It seemed to bring a healing to his heart that he could be accepted by people once again. The old man had listened and encouraged David to not let his past get in his way. After all, he had served his time, and he was sorry. God had forgiven him and washed him of the stain of it. It was time to move on, to find his call in this life of newly found freedom.

The farmer had let him off just across the street from the place called 'Riverside Park,' and now David wandered aimlessly around, taking in the place he had been told to come to. It was a very large park in the middle of a fairly large city. The strange thing about it was all the people who lived in the park. The farmer had said that there were many people who were considered 'homeless.' They had lost jobs and homes, and with no where else to go had ended up in this park. The city had fought to have them removed, but many had come against this action without a plan for some type of housing. So far it was tied up in a 'lot of red tape,' while more and more people entered the homeless ranks.

As David walked about he was amazed to see entire families living in cardboard boxes and makeshift tent homes with tarps and plastic going in different directions. Little children crying and playing along side winos'drunk on cheap wine. Men and women dressed in finer clothes than some others who looked totally out of place with the little box homes, and tents that they lived in. He could see that all types of people were affected by this state of 'homelessness.'

Standing out starkly though, were the hollow eyes always looking back at him, so much hopeless sorrow. Even in prison he did not see so much hopelessness. These people, why some of them looked as though the end of life would easily be an encouragement. In fact the old farmer had told him that suicide was being committed sometimes daily by these desperate people. David guessed the old farmer had read that statistic in the newspaper.

As he walked along, he could not help but pray. Silently he called out to the Lord of his life. *What would You have me to do Lord? I see such a need for Your salvation among these lost one's. Please use me. Show me how to help them, Jesus! The answer does not lie with the world, that I know, it is with You. You are the only Way, the Truth, and the Life for these who are on the brink of death. I'll do anything You say. Just show me.* David cried out from the depths of his heart. He felt as though he were back in prison as he looked around, but in a different way; these people were imprisoned by circumstance, by fear and by sin.

After several hours and as nightfall approached, David found his own little cardboard house, and settled in for the night. He felt so much, fear welled up within him as he thought of all the people who needed help. He felt so helpless as he took in all of their circumstances. *Well, Lord,*

David spoke quietly to himself, *I can only have faith that as You have brought me here, You also have a plan of action. Although I must confess, I feel very overwhelmed by this place and all the need that surrounds me.* David sighed deeply and closed his eyes to sleep.

Putiel was there. As David slept, the angel came and spoke with the man in a dream. "David, stay here and live among these people. Listen to their stories and learn from them. Love them as you have been loved by the Savior. Be as one of them, and let the light of the dear Savior's love shine through you. In two more days, you will meet a woman named SaraJean. She will come to drink at a nearby fountain. Tell her of Jesus. She will hear you and respond. Even in this place, a church can be started. Read the Ancient book, of how the Apostle Paul went into the city and waited for the Spirit to guide him to where the ministry was to begin. Many of these people here will be as a light for the whole nation, and as a testimony of the power of the gospel of Jesus Christ to save the lost. This place shall be part of the last great outpouring upon the non Jews. Even now a remnant of believers who have not submitted to the Antichrist are being prepared to come here and help with the ministry that is about to come forth in this forlorn place.

Remember, it was the stable where the birth of Christ took place. It is still the 'stable' places where the people least expect a move of God, that is where the birthing of the gospel message often is brought forth."

"Also know this, there are a group of elderly women, who live not far from this place, they have prayed and petitioned the heavens for this place and the outpouring of the Spirit that is about to occur. Their prayers have gone up day and night before the throne of God, and He has not turned a deaf ear to them. I tell you this, those women, hidden away as they are in their little prayer closets are some of the greatest Saints upon this earth. It is their persistence and unceasing prayers that have brought this great outpouring that even now is being flooded over this area in the spiritual realm."

"Before I leave your sleep David, there is one last thing I must tell you." Putiel smiled as he spoke the next words, for he knew that his charge would not expect the possibility of it to happen to him. "You will meet a young woman in the near future, David. She will be your wife. She is even now being prepared for the ministry that the two of you will share. The Lord truly restores all that the worm has eaten, son."

The angel gently eased out of David's sleep, looking at his slumbering charge, he saw a smile upon the man's face. "So you heard that last part, did you!" the angel laughed to himself.

Chapter Seventeen

Susan needed to be alone with her thoughts. *How strange, I'm in some sort of dream world and I want to be alone.* She wasn't sure whether that would be okay, so she looked over at the angel who had remained with her constantly.

Adaiah knew Susan's thoughts and responded to them. "You have need to be alone, this is not unusual child. So much has been shown to you and I know that it is much to grasp. The time will come when you will be able to absorb all that you are learning, but for now we must continue on the journey set ahead of us. Let me pray for you and strengthen you, little one." The angel reached out his arm toward his charge.

Susan felt the strength that the angel was imparting to her, and she relaxed into it. She felt like she was breathing some type of energized air. A calmness and peace began to envelop her entire being as she breathed the essence of the mist that the angel seemed to be blowing over her. She smelled flowers, fragrances of lavender and spice, she thought of hillsides covered with flowers and beautiful ocean sunsets, and felt as though she were actually there in the scenes. The beauty of all creation seemed enhanced or enlarged somehow to her senses. She wanted to ask the angel about it, but did not want to disturb the beauty of it all. The more she relaxed, the more she drifted away with the fragrance of it. Until she felt that she was adrift on a pillow like cloud, amid a sea of gentle cleansing breezes and soft flowers.

After what seemed like hours, the angel spoke. "A little bit of heaven goes a long way, child." The angel paused while Susan continued to float along. "Remember what the Master said? 'Eye has not seen, nor has anyone heard of the things which He has prepared for those who love Him'. These are gifts to you little child, His gifts of love that you should enter His rest."

Susan felt herself return to reality, at least as much as possible in this strange dream state that she found herself in. "Could I have that happen when I'm awake too?" she inquired innocently of the angel.

"Yes, of course you can. The Spirit is always willing to fill you with His rest. All that you need to do is to receive it. Sometimes you may experience different manifestations of His presence, but always you will receive from Him if you ask. The Spirit gives you the new wine of His presence, to refresh you and help you to stay focused upon Him."

"I am ready to proceed now, it is like I've been regenerated somehow." Susan smiled warmly at the angel. She felt as though she was glowing with the light of the Spirit.

"Indeed you are ready child, and we must continue for there is much that you have to learn." The angel escorted his charge to her next lesson.

Janna sat next to Susan as she lie on her bed. Looking at the form of the dear girl who had become like a daughter to them, she fought tears away. "It is so hard to have faith sometimes, Lord. What if she is not okay? What if something is wrong with her?"

She thought of the last few days since Paul had told her about his encounter with the angel. She was feeling as if her life would never be the same again. She knew that Paul was right in saying that God moves in mysterious ways. She was also glad that she had been reading a book about past revivals and had found that a person going into this deep presence of the Spirit was not unusual. In fact, when she read about it, she had even wondered what happened to a person's body while they were sleeping. Well, now she knew. She smiled wryly at her charge. Susan was like a little baby, needing attention for all her bodily functions. Janna saw that the nurses training that she had years before was useful now. She fed Susan and kept her clean, but otherwise there was no communication between them, it was strange. Her body would sometime twitch and shake, as if she were encountering something that caused her to fear, or the girl would cry or moan as if in pain. Then, just recently, Janna was sure that she smelled flowers as Susan laughed. Occasionally, the girl would speak aloud. Her eyes open as if looking at her, but unseeing. When this happened, she would quickly grab her notebook and take notes as she had been instructed to do by Paul.

The notebook now rested in her lap, and she pondered what was written in it. "No help in the arm of the flesh," she spoke a portion of the book aloud. *It is true that we can't help ourselves, but it is so hard to admit. I have been taught all my life that I have to do my part, that God expects my input. Over and over I have been taught that 'faith without works is dead', although I never quite understood the meaning of faith. They always seemed to skip over that part. I know that Abraham believed God when a son was promised to his barren wife, and God called him a father of faith. But Abraham didn't do anything but believe what God said. Maybe all my striving to change things in my own power is not faith, and just believing God when He gives me a promise is faith. My, but this is confusing to my religious mind. It is much easier for me to relieve my conscience by doing 'things' rather than just standing on faith. Maybe that is why I don't see any power in my life.*

As Janna was thinking these thoughts, Dizahab, Janna's angel was close by ministering truth to her heart. "You are called to be a daughter of faith, Ebiasaph. You are a gatherer, and I have been given to help you abound in the golden anointing of the Lord."

The angel held his hands over her and opened them. Gold dust, as pure and fine as the mist of fog, began to infiltrate the atmosphere of the room. It swirled and floated gently in the atmosphere, light and clear, sweet and simple, it landed gently upon Janna.

Janna felt the presence of the Spirit. The whole room began to glow in a soft yellow hue. This was not the first time that she had this experience, for it had come to her over and over since the first day of her baptism in the Spirit. She loved the peace and beauty of her Lord, and felt that being in His presence for all of eternity would be the only true happiness that she could ever know. Softly, she began to sing a song without known words. A tongue of angelic language came forth as she sang and worshipped her Savior. Janna relaxed in the atmosphere of God's love, knowing that this is what made everything worthwhile. "I am so glad that I do not have to wait until heaven to experience the kingdom of Heaven Lord!" Janna spoke out loud, laughing as she spoke. Then she continued the song, and enjoyed the heavenly communication between Father and daughter.

Dizahab also sang along with his charge. If listening ears had been present, two voices would have been heard. Now it was just the two of them, and the bodily form of Susan, gone for a season to places unseen.

Chapter Eighteen

Paul sat quietly at his desk, staring into the space around him, eyes unseeing. His thoughts were again on the moment of heavenly visitation that occurred a few nights ago. Every since that night, a strangeness pervaded Paul's very soul. He felt as though he were undone. It was as if a hot, searing torch had gone through his every thought and motivation in life and exposed the raw nerves of every intention. He knew this was right. The only way that he could be a vessel of pure use was if he were cleansed with the refiner's soap. It felt as though he was being scrubbed from the inside out. He thought of the Disciple known as Peter, in the Ancient book. Peter was always pushing to be and do all that he could, but his zeal often got him in trouble. Once Peter saw the Master out on a lake, walking on the water. Asking that He too might join Jesus out on the water, Peter had boldly gone where no man had ever gone. At first he walked, but then an inward truth of his being came forth. Fear. He was afraid. It was a hard lesson for Peter, thought Paul. Having his interior self brought out in such a way. And yet, how else could our flesh be dealt with. Exposure was the only way, this Paul knew for sure. No matter what the cost to the flesh, no matter how painful.

Paul knew that if he were to serve the Lord, as he was instructed, then he must be emptied of self. The Spirit within him had told him to prepare his vessel for an infilling of the power that was needed to go forward. In the past, Paul had been taught that the infilling, or 'baptism of the Spirit' as it was called, had been given the moment he asked for it. This infilling was manifest, they taught, by his speaking in tongues. Paul had often questioned this teaching. He wondered about the power that was supposed to accompany this 'baptism.' Since he had not experienced the power, maybe he was not truly baptized?

"Even though I do not understand all of these things, one thing I do know; I need to receive a baptism of power for the type of work that I have been called to do. Or if I have already received it, then I need faith to believe in it. I know that this power does not reside in men, but in the Spirit of God." Paul spoke his thoughts aloud to the seemingly empty room.

Taralah was there. He was ready, at the Master's word, to begin instilling faith in the man. "Anaiah, you are so close. By His grace, by His empowering presence, you are saved from yourself. Faith is how you receive this grace-power. And faith is a gift of God, given to those who will seek after it. Faith cannot be earned through outworking flesh. Faith is believing in the unseen realms more than what you can see with your human eyes. To be a man of this faith, you must leave behind all reliance on the earth and her ways. You cannot rely on the temporal things and be full of the eternal gifts.You must leave behind all hope in this place, in the flesh, and put your entire hope upon the Father. He is the One who originates this faith, the One who can bring it to fruition." The angel blew his breath of spiritual wisdom over the man.

Paul felt the ministry of the Spirit speak clearly to his heart. He began to see anew that His salvation was not something that happened a long time ago. It was happening even now. He was in the process of being saved. He shuddered at how many times he had referred to himself as 'saved,' implying that all the work was done. In truth, his salvation was much like human growth, it was a daily affair.

"Lord, I'm so thankful for Your patience with me. You are so wonderful. Thank You for the truth that You speak to my heart. Show me Your ways! Guide me into Your truth! Instill Your life into me that I might resemble You in all that I am! And let all the glory, honor and praise be Yours for this marvelous work that You do in me." Paul spoke aloud to the Master of Life who always listened for the prayer of His chosen ones.

Chapter Nineteen

David sat cross-legged on the grass. The sun was bright and hot. He felt himself breathe deeply of the fresh, sparkling air. He felt so thankful for this life he now found himself in. *It's funny*, he thought, *here I am, living in a homeless Park, and feeling more thankful for it than anything I've ever experienced. This is what my Savior has done for me. I've never felt such a freedom before! To be able to enjoy simple things, like the sun warming me up in the early morning, and the fresh air that I breathe, it's wonderful.* David smiled warmly to himself.

"A penny for your thoughts?" Jess, the man sitting next to David spoke aloud, breaking the stillness of the moment. Jess, and his wife Trisha, was a couple that David had befriended his first day in the park. They had lost everything they owned and ended up living in the park with their two small children. Jess had been hurt in a construction accident that eventually caused him to lose his job, and things spiraled downward as medical expenses drove them to desperation.

David smiled at Jess with a sort of childish grin. "I was just thinking how beautiful it is today, Jess."

"You sure are a strange sort. If I didn't know any better, I would say that you enjoy living here. But no one in his right mind could actually enjoy living here. So what really put that smile on your face, David. Have you got a secret?" Jess teased David back. They were becoming fast friends.

"That's for me to know and you to find out." David teased back. He wanted to begin sharing his Savior's story with this man, but had not yet felt the leading of the Spirit. He thought of the saying in the Ancient book that said, *Jesus only did what His Father was doing.* Jesus always waited on the Father to open the way before Him, and David wanted this same type of relationship with the Father. He knew that the day was here when he would meet the woman at the fountain. Today it was to be, even as the dream had told him. He wondered to himself if she would also be the woman he was to marry. Time would tell. Even now, he sat in full view of the fountain that he had been shown in his dream. It was a fountain where many of the homeless people came to fill their water jugs so that they could have drinking and cooking water at their campsites.

"That smile reminds me of the time that I first met my wife, Trisha. Maybe you have a girl. Is that it David? Have you met someone?" Jess teased David, breaking into his private thoughts. Jess was smiling as if he knew David's 'secret.'

At just that same moment, David felt the quickening of the Spirit within him. Time to get up and go over to the fountain. "Not that I know of, old man. Keep on guessing. I'm going after some fresh water. See ya later." David shook Jess's hand as he got up to leave.

He walked slowly over to the fountain, observing the area around him. No one was close by. He took a long, cool drink then sat down on the grass nearby. Then, from behind him, a woman who looked to be about 35 approached the fountain with a large jug to fill. She absently put the jug under the fountain and turned on the water as if her thoughts were a million miles away.

"Hi," David spoke aloud as the woman stood there.

"Oh, hello. I didn't see you there. Did you want to get a drink before I start filling this jug?" The woman responded back at David a little awkwardly. "I didn't mean to hog the fountain."

"If you knew about the water that I have access to, you would be asking me for a drink," David spoke pointedly to the woman. He looked intently into her eyes as he spoke, as if he was able to see right into her soul.

She took a step back and looked around. "You aren't trying to sell me some kind of drug, are you? I don't do that kind of thing. Maybe you should get out of here." She looked over toward a group of men behind David.

David turned and saw who she looked at. He smiled and repeated the offer. "I have pure water, and I'm not talking about drugs. This water that I speak of can quench the very thirst of life that cries out within you. It is a healing water that purifies the whole soul."

"Let me see this water. You have no container. How can you have water that does these things? I have never heard of it." The pale haired woman walked closer toward David as he sat on the ground. She peered around him as if he might be hiding something from her.

"Go, call your husband. Ask him if he wants some of this water." David spoke quietly to the woman as she looked around him.

As he spoke these last words, the woman seemed to breathe in as if startled. She looked back at David intently as he was looking at her. "I don't have a husband!" she responded almost fearfully.

"That is true. You have left your husband and are living with another man. In fact you have had several husbands, and this one is not your husband. What are you looking for?"

David perceived the woman with an ability to look deep into her soul where the cry of her heart had remained unanswered for a decade.

"How do you know these things? Are you a prophet? I've read of it in the Ancient book as a child, but I never really understood those things. How do you know of my search? I have never spoken of it to anyone except the voiceless God I hope is up there somewhere." She gestured up toward the sky.

"God is not voiceless, SaraJean. He is present with His people because of His son who He sent to make a way of salvation. He has heard your cries and sent me to help you find Him. He saw your need for love. You have tried to fill the void in your heart with a man. Yet you have never been satisfied, have you?" David continued to speak with the power and light of the Spirit within him.

"How do you know my name?" The woman looked even closer at David, as if she could somehow see whether or not he was true. Then she continued to answer him. "No, I came over here wanting to somehow run away from the man that I slept with last night. He was another mistake. I feel so empty inside." She began to cry as David reached out his hand to touch her arm. "I've really screwed up my life. I really just want to end it all." The woman spoke dejectedly. "Is there really any hope?"

"I have met the One true hope. He came to me while I was in prison and saved me from killing myself. He will come to you also, all you need to do is ask. He came to wash you clean inside out with the only thing that can help you, the blood that he shed in your place. Come over here under this tree and let me tell you His story. You'll be glad that you did!" David pointed over toward some close by trees and started to walk to them. The woman followed like a little lost puppy who finally found someone to love it.

Chapter Twenty

Meanwhile, Susan continued to learn about the Truth from the Spirit's perspective. She had been brought into a new realm of this training where she was able to see the true hopelessness of man's condition. After leaving the river and John the Baptist she was whisked into the heavens by the angel Adaiah. She found herself in a great courtroom of celestial makeup, in that it was huge as the sky and seemed to go on forever. There were angels of every make and size, with rows of seats that surrounded a center stage. The seats rose upward into the air for layer after layer, and yet somehow each seat and occupant was close enough for her to distinctly make out the fine features of facial expression. It was as if the distance was clearer somehow, and there were not the normal distortions of space that she was accustomed to on the earth. At the center of the stage or main area was a large marble like floor that expanded about one hundred feet in diameter, and centered in the front of the room was a very large mahogany type table with a golden throne behind it. The table was carved with detailed pictures from the creation of earth. Susan recognized scenes from the garden of Eden, the pictures told the story in wonderful detail, from the beginning to the fall of mankind as he chose the forbidden fruit over true life. On each side of the table, surrounding the perimeter of the marble floor were smaller chairs also made of gold, twelve on each side. These chairs were occupied by glorious beings, she was not sure if they were angelic or human, though they were human in size. She perceived that they were some type of lesser judges or elders.

It seemed that all the people in the seats above the center stage were some sort of heavenly beings and aside from her the only other human being present was the poor pitiful leper that John had washed in the river earlier.

The leper was standing in front of the mahogany table as if on trial. He was even more wounded than what she had seen before at the river. As he stood there, a great Judge came into the court. His appearance was like the dawning of the sun, bright rays filled the entire room, shining on each person and object in the room with a brilliancy that was beyond anything she had ever imagined. The light made it difficult to see his form, yet she somehow understood that He represented all truth and justice. As He entered the room, bright, vibrating light fell upon each occupant of the room, exposing every detail of their makeup, causing the angels to glow and pulse with power and glory. The air in the room seemed alive, as if each molecule was pulsing with the glory of this great Judge. Susan could not help but breathe deeply of the golden air that was filling the room with His great Presence. The breath in her body seemed to fill each cell with understanding, somehow causing her to understand unspeakable mysteries. It was as though she was a living part of Him, belonging to Him in every way possible, like a drop of water falling into a river. She felt the glory, the power and the majesty of this awesome God, and bowed her head low at His thunderous presence.

The Judge carried golden scales in His hand and He held it over the poor leper. As He did this, the scale tipped over to one side, as if heaped full with no counter balance. Then the Judge set the scales down on the table and sat on the throne behind the table. He began to speak and His voice was like a thundering river. Susan shook visibly as the Judge spoke, His words beating within her heart with truth and power.

"The sentence is eternal death for man. He has made himself unclean with the wickedness of good and evil knowledge. His soul is a contagious disease that cannot be brought into the eternal bliss of the heavens. He contaminates all that he comes in contact with. His condition is incurable. Is there any remedy for man's condition?"

The voice of the Judge echoed throughout the room, up into the sky, and out into all time, from the beginning to the far reaches of creation. Then, as the echo of His voice disappeared into the recesses of time, silence permeated the entire court and the heavens also. The celestial beings looked at one another with questioning looks, and Susan seemed to know the question they asked without hearing the words.

"Is there any remedy for sin sick man? Is there any hope to be found in all existence? Or shall eternal separation exit this poor creature from all that is pure and light?"

Upon hearing these words, Susan fell to her knees and sobbed deeply, her chest heaving with gut wrenching horror. In her heart she knew that this man was the representation for all of mankind. It was her! And it was every human who had ever existed. As the agony over her true condition began to press into her heart, she trembled with fear at the thought of eternal separation from all light. Somehow she knew what it would be like to be cast into the outer darkness. She could feel it coming after her. It was like a great open mouth, with a black hole in the midst of it. To be swallowed up in that hole, or chasm, would mean a loss of life to the degree that all substance would be void. There would be no form of self, only empty naked darkness, where the soul would ever seek a place of rest, but without an answer. As it was shown to her what this void represented, the writing from the Ancient book came to her as if written upon the very skin of her existence. "In Him we live and move and have our being."

The answer to her dilemma! Hope began to stir within the deep recesses of her spirit. Even as this awareness was given to her, a stirring among the celestial beings was taking place also. In the midst of the courtroom floor the Judge had laid the decree of eternal separation. It was a scroll that had the judgment written upon it. As he laid it there, the Judge had put his ring to it and sealed it closed with His stamp of authority. All the celestial beings began to cry out, and Susan joined them.

"Who can break the seal? Is there any who can take the judgment off of the man? Where is Hope?" They began to chant as they cried for mercy upon the man and his sentence. The cry somehow followed the echo of the judgment, out into the recesses of eternity it went. Then afterwards, silence. Silence that was waiting for God, for help, for hope. All were waiting.

The little footsteps seemed to echo from a long way off, "clip, clop, clip, clop." The sound grew with the nearness of the approaching creature. The entire room seemed to hold its breath as the sound drew closer upon them. Then, a little white lamb appeared in the midst of the courtroom. It walked over to the scroll and circled around it. Soft little bleats came from its muzzle, as if inquiring to the message written on the scroll. Then, as if the lamb understood the message, it walked over to the scroll and began to eat it. As the lamb ate, it began to bleed as if it had been cut at its throat. Just as suddenly, Susan felt herself being removed from the heavenly scene and thrust back into the earth's atmosphere.

Once again she stood at the river's edge, and before her stood the Baptist. Another man was coming to be baptized, yet he was not a man, he was the lamb from the heavenly scene she had just watched unfold. She did not know how she knew this, it was a revelation to her, and to the Baptist as he saw the man coming. John knelt before him, his face showing the awe that he felt at that moment. "Behold the Lamb of God who takes away the sin of the world!"

Chapter Twenty-One

S usan realized at that moment that she understood the words of the Baptist, even though she did not understand the language.

"Since you have been in the heavenly realm, the veil of language has been removed from you." The angel was once again at her side.

"How is it that you know my thoughts without me speaking them?" Susan inquired, "What do you mean by the veil of language?"

"Communication was meant to be pure. Before the tower of Babel was built, all men were able to communicate as we do in the heavens, with one language, and purity of words. It was used against the Most High God when man desired to follow Lucifer and become as great as God. Since they had become unified in their purpose, it would have caused an annihilation of all the inhabitants of the earth again, as in the flood, if they had been allowed to build any further. It was for their own sake that the Father blessed them with the veil. By concealing their communication, they were no longer able to be unified and the power of the deceiver was broken over them. Pure communication is having the veil lifted off of your hearing. You do not need to understand a language to know the meaning of the words because you are hearing with spiritual ears. Many times you have felt the inability to express yourself, as all mankind does, this is due to the veil. Now, while you are in this place of learning it has been lifted. In the future, it will be lifted as the Remnant begins to preach the gospel to the lost. It was removed for a short time during the early church when Peter was preaching and thousands heard the word preached in their own language. Unfortunately, the veil was only lifted as long as the church was following the Holy Spirit. When the Antichrist spirit came in and the church entered into the dark ages, it was lost. The Remnant will bring in the fulness of the Spirit once again, although there are places in the world that are even now operating in this freedom. Now you must continue to watch and learn." The angel gestured toward the river where the interaction between the Baptist and the Savior was taking place.

The Savior came to John and raised him to his feet. "You must baptize me!" He looked intently at the man. "It is necessary for the fulfilment of all things." He spoke aloud to the resistance of the Baptist. John was shaking his head and asking that he be the one to be to be baptized.

"I have waited. You are coming to baptize with fire. I want this baptism!" John plead with the Son of God. He grimaced as his hearts greatest desire was not being granted to him.

Then Jesus took John by the shoulders and looked deeply into his eyes. His eyes spoke unheard words to the man that caused tears to fall down the Baptist's cheek.

Then quietly, submissively, the Baptist obeyed. He held the Son and carried Him downward into the muddy river Jordan. The Lamb of God began the journey of redemption for all who are lost. He took the scroll, the Judgment, and He received it unto His own flesh. The outward example of

His soon coming death was shown as He submitted and went under the water.

Susan watched in wonder. "He came willingly, didn't He?" she asked the angel.

"Just as you saw the little lamb eat the scroll, the Son of God has voluntarily chosen to be the One whom all judgment is cast upon. The judgment cannot be simply erased. It must be paid to the full. The payment is death. Man must die for his sin. There is no other way for the judgment to be satisfied. When death first entered man as Adam and Eve sinned in the garden, their blood became impure, disease is carried in the blood, the disease of sin. Jesus Christ came from God the Father, sinless and pure and only His blood is perfect and able to wipe away the curse from all mankind. The Son has come in the form of a man. He will become as the poor leper, He will take all the sin of all mankind and carry the judgment for it. He will die." Adaiah spoke with a sadness that Susan did not quite understand. She wanted to grasp what the angel was feeling, but could not cross the barrier that separated her from the celestial being.

"You are the one's for whom He gave up all His heavenly prosperity. He is the King of all Kings, the Lord of Glory, and He gave all up to enter into the frailty of human flesh. We angels are awed by His love. You cannot understand this from your earthly point of view. You do not understand all that He gave up to come here. You have not seen all that He is!" The angel spoke with such an air of sorrow that Susan wished she were not of the human race who was responsible for such a cost.

"I do not blame you! Not at all. It is just that I know of the cost. It causes me to want to bow forever and worship Him with all of my might just to mention what He has done for mankind." The angel spoke tenderly with Susan, easing her guilty conscience.

"I'm sorry that it has caused you so much pain. I know that it is good for me to come here and learn. Thank you for taking me on this journey, for being my guide." She spoke sincerely to the heavenly being, her eyes sparkling with unshed tears.

The angel turned her again to the scene at the river. As the Son of God came up from the water, a loud voice spoke into the atmosphere around them as if a great thunderbolt. "This is My Son! I am well pleased with Him!" As the voice spoke, a beautiful white dove came from the heavens and landed on the shoulder of Jesus. Then as the Son of God inhaled deeply, the dove seemed to disappear as if only an apparition. With this gesture He walked out of the river and headed into the wilderness, alone.

Susan started to follow Jesus, but the angel took her arm and kept her back. "We cannot go where He is going. He must meet His enemy alone. You too will meet the same enemy, but you will never be alone. He is the conqueror, and you are more than a conqueror because of what He is able to overcome for you. You have read of this encounter in the Ancient book. This will suffice for now. We must continue our journey." The angel spread his wings and with Susan lifted off to another place, another time.

Chapter Twenty-Two

Paul and Janna continued to live their quiet lives despite the fact that a young woman lie in a trance-like state in their home. So far they had been spared any questions regarding Susan's whereabouts, and they were very thankful for that. They had spoken among themselves what they would say if questioned, but preferred not to have any questions asked if possible. It seemed that God was in control and so far. They had not needed to concern themselves with it. They continued to attend the same church, despite the rejection that they suffered. Paul felt they must continue to seek fellowship as much as possible. This was an unusual Sunday though. They had gone to the meeting, but the lesson that was being taught was more about honoring man than God. Paul felt as though he was hearing the devil himself preach. *What happened to preaching about Jesus and the simple gospel truth? The people needed to hear about the freedom of the gospel, not how to conform to the image of the beast.* Paul thought to himself.

Paul was finding it very difficult to keep from shouting out in the same manner as Jesus had done against the Pharisee's, *You whitewashed hypocrites! Why do you burden the people with heaviness, and not lift the load off of their backs? They look at you as if you carry all hope and truth in who you are, only because you have not been transparent about your own need. You focus on yourselves as if you have attained something by your own righteousness, then compare yourselves with the sheep and leave them wondering how to be more like you. Can't you see you are only making images of yourselves? And yet you reject all who would stand up and be different as if they were some sort of devil.* Of course he knew that this would be unacceptable and held his tongue. Instead he went and sat in the car while Janna spoke with her friends after the service was over.

As he sat there, he remembered a dream that he had recently. In the dream, a snake had appeared on the water of a lake. The snake came to shore and emerged very large. Out of its belly grew three horse's heads.

He had contemplated the meaning of the dream and spoke of it to Janna. They knew that the snake represented Satan and horses represented strength. Then, last night, Janna had read something to him about how the enemy works as the Accuser of the Brethren. It said that he was like "a triple braided cord of three stronghold spirits." The Religious spirit, the Political spirit and the Control spirit. He felt that the three horses' heads might be the three spirits controlling the errant church. The Antichrist spirit was gaining ground and it seemed that any who got in its way was removed from the scene.

Paul thought on these things for quite some time, then as the parking lot emptied he began to wonder if Janna was okay. He decided to go into the church and check on her. As he approached the front door, the Pastor came toward him.

"Paul, I've been meaning to speak with you about some things," the man quickly approached Paul. "It seems that there has been a problem with you and your family attending this church." The man seemed irritated with Paul.

"We are not really interested in the type of teachings that you pursue. There have been some complaints that you have been teaching a bible study at your house that does not quite agree with our doctrinal statements. Perhaps you might be better suited to find fellowship elsewhere." The Pastor eyed Paul keenly, his eyes narrowing as he spoke.

"I've tried to explain about the study before, but you said I should just do what I felt was best. All that we study is the Ancient Book and how to live fully as a Christian in these dark days." Paul replied sincerely. "What could be wrong with that? How does that interfere with your doctrinal statement?" Paul chose his words carefully.

"Paul, that's just it, you feel that these are 'dark' days and we just don't agree with you. The church has never been greater. Thousands are beings touched by God, there is a unity among all faiths that has never existed before. It is not time to put fear into man, but it is time to build. We can be greater than any other church period in history. We could usher in a new age. We are becoming more godlike than we have ever been. One day there will no longer be separation between Muslims and Christians, between the Jews and any other faith. We all have truth and are meant to live in universal light. You try to bring a gloom and doom theology in our midst and it isn't right. I want you to either resign from the church, or read some of the books I've been teaching out of. Maybe if you could study something besides that old Ancient book, something that's not so outdated, it might shed a little light on you. What do you say?" The Pastor tried to smile innocently, but the smile sent chills through Paul. He felt as if he had been doused with cold water.

"Don't you see that what you are teaching is New Age doctrine? How can you agree with this stuff?" Paul tried to reach through the hard heart of the man. Yet he saw in the man's face that he was getting nowhere. "What about preaching the gospel of Jesus Christ? How do you explain

His death and resurrection? How can you leave that behind?" Paul asked cautiously.

"Paul, you must know that some of the things that we have believed since childhood are myths and fairy tales. When I was little, I was often told that there would be some sort of rapture where all the Christians would be taken away from this terrible world. I remember asking my Mother what would happen to all the people who would be left, the one's who didn't have the same belief as us. I was told that they would suffer terribly, and there would be no one to help them find any peace. All my life this has bothered me. Now I know that this is a fantasy someone concocted from the Ancient book meant to scare people into believing in Jesus. I have found a truth that calls all men brothers and honors great men among them, including Jesus. He was a great man! He gave us many valuable lessons that we must never forget. But He is dead and now it is time to honor other great men who also have things to teach us. We must be open minded. Look at where we are in history. We have the ability to talk with each other without language interference via the computer. Can't you see the possibilities for global peace? If you can't, then you are blind. Either conform to what our mission is, or leave. That is the choice, Paul. We can not have any more of your one-sided doctrine running loose and offending people, now can we?" The Pastor eyed Paul with an unrelenting look that made Paul shudder. He knew that it was time to leave the Church. God had other plans for his life, and now it was upon him to choose.

"I cannot deny my Savior and His ever present Life and Resurrection power that abides within me. I am sorry for you! You have been deceived by the Antichrist spirit and have lost your way. I will pray for you, and for your restoration to the One True Faith!" Paul felt hot tears stinging his eyes. It hurt him to see this man so completely lose his way.

"Don't bother! Just take your self-righteous self and family and stay away from us! Do you hear me?" The Pastor was visibly upset, his face was red and his brows furrowed tightly, his voice raised to a yelling pitch. He had a darkness in his eyes that caused Paul to catch his breath and wonder at how the man could be so possessed by such evil.

"Good-bye." Paul turned and walked away.

Darkon sat next to the Pastor and laughed his hideous demon laugh. "I love it when a Christian gets it from one of ours. It feels so fine! That Paul-man is nothing but trouble. I'm going to make sure that he is the topic of all the gossips for the next few days. Maybe something really degrading, like molesting a child or something like that. These stupid humans always believe anything they hear, and they always agree with the accusation without ever attempting to see if there is any merit to it. I love the way they cut each other apart, I get a full meal out of the flesh that is exposed in even some of the most 'righteous' saints. Ha Ha Ha."

Darkon lifted his bat-like wings and with a frenzy of flapping he flew off to take care of the ugly gossip that was about to ruin Paul and Janna's delicate reputation in the wayward little Church.

Chapter Twenty-Three

David had continued to meet with SaraJean almost daily. He taught her from the Ancient book and she listened with all of her heart. She was like the dried up soil receiving a summer rain, the teachings seemed to sit on top and then slowly penetrate her being like life-giving fluid. David loved to watch her face as he gave the lessons, she was so willing to learn. Several others had also joined in the daily study, one or two each day and now there were about twenty people sitting and listening to him read. Most of his readings were taken from the part of the Ancient book recording Jesus' walk on the earth and what He spoke. To these poor people, it was an acceptance that few of them heard anywhere. The words were life and light to them.

Even now as he looked around, David could see that this woman, SaraJean, was having quite an impact upon the other homeless people at the park. She was the reason so many joined the study. She had such a peace and light about her that was very noticeable, especially in light of how she was before.

More than anything, though, David was thankful for all that he was learning. It seemed that every time he read to these people, a new understanding of what the teachings in the Ancient book really meant came to him. He began to see the profound love that God has for all people, and how willing He is to give His love to all who will come and seek after it. He saw how Jesus came in the simplicity of life and showed how to really live. God is the Father of every man or woman who would come to Him through the Son and receive Him.

David also saw that the Son of God not only moved through words, but also in power. He constantly demonstrated the Fathers love toward the insecure masses of fallible humanity by acts of divine power that brought healing and freedom to many. David wondered to himself if he also should begin to call out to the Lord for these same demonstrations of power to occur in their midst. He knew that the people were desperate for more than just words spoken in wisdom. If the wisdom was accompanied by demonstration of creative power, then he knew the people would receive more than a form of godliness, but also the resurrection power that brought true change of character.

That night as David prepared for bed, he prayed aloud. "Father, please reveal Yourself to these people in any way that You might have for them to receive all that You are and have for them. I'm a simple man. I have so little understanding of the supernatural realm that Your Son moved so freely in, and yet I see that it is Your way for all Your sons and daughters. Send help Lord! Amen."

Putiel sat quietly beside David as the prayer burst forth from the man's lips. "Yes, it is time for you to meet a fellow worker of the Remnant. It is time for the beginning of the last great outpouring upon this land. I will go and arrange it now." The angel lifted his wings high over the man and with a smile of encouragement he disappeared into the celestial realm that was his sphere. "Now to speak with Taralah about the meeting between Anaiah and Jediael, where power meets light."

It was late and Paul was sitting alone in his living room contemplating all that had taken place that day. It was two days since his encounter with the pastor at the Church, and his rejection by him. On Monday the phone had started to ring with accusations against Paul. One woman had spoken with Janna and told her that Paul had tried to molest her daughter in a back room at the Church. Janna was very upset and asked the woman how and when all this was supposed to have taken place. The woman did not have any detailed answers, but did tell Janna that she had notified the authorities. "Paul will pay for his crimes! You will see!" the woman had angrily shouted in the mouthpiece of the phone before hanging up.

Then on Tuesday, the police had come over and asked Paul to come to the station to answer questions about some allegations that had been brought against him. At the station he was treated as though he were some sort of criminal. Paul had prayed that God would give him wisdom in his answers and that Christ's light would shine through him in this situation.

Even as he had prayed, he felt the peace of God begin to flow over him and take away all the fear. A calming river of the Spirit seemed to be flowing over him and he felt himself being carried in it even as he answered the questions that were being roughly thrown at him.

After a whole afternoon of questioning, the detectives admitted that they had nothing upon which to base any charges against Paul and let him go home. Even with that though, they sent him away knowing that they were "going to watch him like a hawk."

When he arrived home, he found Janna in a state of near panic. She had been inundated with telephone calls warning her to leave Paul before her and the girls were hurt. Apparently the woman who had made the first accusations against Paul had called everyone in the church and warned them about Paul being some sort of demented child-molester and wife-beater. Janna was feeling very shocked at the way everyone seemed to believe this woman without any shred of evidence.

"How can they judge you so quickly? They don't even ask my opinion, they just burst forth with their judgments without even a trial or any questioning. It is as if they choose to believe the worst the moment they hear it." She cried out to Paul with a look of disbelief on her face.

"Remember what they said about our Lord Jesus. He was also rejected and accused wrongly. He warned us that if they rejected Him, they would also reject us. We must keep our focus, Janna. I know that this is the work of the enemy. It all started with the encounter at Church on Sunday. The enemy wants to stop us in our tracks. He knows that God is about to move powerfully and he is afraid of it. He will stop at nothing until he sees that we have been put out of commission. You must remember that he cannot touch us without a foothold into our lives. Do not allow room for bitterness in your heart against the wrongdoing that has come against us. The enemy knows that if he can gain a foothold like bitterness in our hearts, then he can use his authority over us. Satan has no power in those who rest totally in the mercy of God. We must pray for our enemies! We must bless those who use us and hurt us! We must walk in purity and keep our way blameless or else the same trap that has overtaken much of the world will take us captive. Remember that Love covers sin." Paul held Janna close as he spoke these life-giving words to her wounded heart and soothed her over with the same peace of God that had been with him all the day.

Janna relaxed deeply into Paul's embrace and thanked God that she had been given such a wise husband. "I have been just as guilty as they have! I have judged them for judging you. I was angry and did not respond in love.

Jesus, please forgive me and help me to have Your love in my heart. I want to be like you, Lord. Please let Your light be my guide!" She breathed deeply of the Love she felt from her Savior. "Thank you Lord for always being here! I love you."

Now, as Paul sat in reflection of all that had happened he could not help but wonder what was next. "I know I'm headed into a new phase of something. God never closes one door without opening another. So here I am Lord. What have You got for me to do now?" Paul spoke and prayed aloud. Even as his prayer ended he knew that the answer was about to be given, evidenced by the changing atmosphere of the room.

"Looks like I'm in for another heavenly visitation." Paul said aloud to the gathering light of celestial origins that was appearing around him.

Chapter Twenty-Four

For what seemed like weeks, Susan had sat at the feet of Jesus as He taught about Love. She was invisible to the people around her, and yet she so easily related to them. Living in a different time, nearly two thousand years in the future had not changed mankind much at all, she thought. How often she had heard of the advanced technology of the twentieth century, and yet really all that there was to show for it was more sophisticated ways of destroying each other.

Jesus taught them that God was Love. To follow after this Love would be the greatest freedom that they could ever possess. It would be worth dying for, and it was definitely worth living for. Over and over He demonstrated the Love of the Father by healing and forgiving, by bringing life and hope over death and despondency.

She was amazed at the words that He spoke. She had read them in the Ancient book, but here they were filled with power and life that she had not known was in them just by reading them. Not that she was unchanged at reading them, she knew that she had received so much from them. Yet here it was different, what with the veil of communication lifted and the purity of the man Jesus, it was as if

His words were more than words. They were creative and powerful.

If only this way of teaching the Ancient book could be taught in our time. She thought to herself. *It would bring so much light to the true meaning of things. So much has been misunderstood. So much has been changed by our human understanding and the darkness that we see everything through. I want the veil to be removed from my understanding Lord!* she wanted to shout aloud and cry out for help, not only for herself, but for her entire generation of lost people.

"You are here for this purpose, little one." The angel at her side spoke. "To be shown these things is not only for you, but it is for the coming times. You must know that you can never teach or speak anything of your own wisdom. Even reading aloud from the Ancient book without the empowering presence of the Holy Spirit will only lead to form and not to the power that changes the hardness of mans' heart." The angel spoke gingerly. "The cries from your generation have reached the thrones of heaven," Adaiah smiled at Susan. "They are not going to find hope in a world that only offers words without power to change. All of the words of man's wisdom put together will not ease the suffering of the human soul, for all these words are only built upon emptiness and death. Jesus is the resurrection and the life, no one comes to the Father by any other means. It is the natural inclination of all men to desire the love of his father. Nothing else will suffice. Unless they are shown the Father, they continue to die hopeless. To your fatherless generation though, it is time to reveal the Father once again. Jesus taught about the Father. He showed the people who the Father is and how much He loves them, and He asks that all His disciples do the same."

"Is that why I have been raised fatherless? To find the true Father?" Susan asked the angel innocently.

"Yes, child, that is part of the reason. He is able to use everything that you experience to bring about the fullness of the gospel in your life. He knows everything about you and how to best teach you and bring you to the place where you can fulfill all that He has for you to do." The angel answered with a smile, evidently enjoying the questions that his charge brought forth.

Then Jesus stood up from His teaching and spoke to His disciples that they should go to the boat and travel to the other side of the lake. Susan looked up to the angel to see what she should do. Knowingly, the angel answered her unspoken question." Go ahead and join them. He knows you are here and He wants to teach you as well."

Susan followed at a short distance, wondering what was up. As they climbed into the boat, she followed Jesus as He made His way across the boat to a place where He could rest. Sitting herself by His side, she waited and watched. She could not help but stare at Jesus while He slept. *He is so ordinary looking, nothing stands out about Him at all, and yet in my heart I know who He is and I am fascinated by Him. I know that this body that He dwells in is temporal and He is eternal, how can He do it?* She thought as she watched Him. Even as He slept, she noticed that a peace and gentleness seemed to exude from His being. Yet as she looked around the boat and watched the others, men at work with oars and sails, it seemed that they had not really grasped just Who was with them.

After a short time the weather became rough. Though the Master slept on, she could see and feel the tension of the men rising. Soon the boat was rising and falling into the crests of the waves as they grew, she herself could not help but feel anxious. The waves were heavy and frothy with the fierce wind pushing them higher and higher. The sky thundered deeply with flashes of lightning bringing strange looks from the men like a strobe light flashing. The air was moist and heavy, the mist thick and wet. The men were working furiously to bail the water that came in with each wave, threatening to fill the boat. Fear was working itself into a frenzy. She wanted to jump up and help, to cry out, to do something.

Then, as if in answer to her own fear, she heard the angel speak. She looked around but could not see him. Again he spoke and she listened. "Look at Him!" came the command.

She felt as if she was in slow motion. At that moment she turned away from all the turmoil around her and looked upon the sleeping Savior. As she looked, slowly at first, then with fullness peace came. She found herself moving closer to Him. *Sweet peace take me now*! She felt her spirit drink in all that was being made available to her. The storm of fear in her own heart was being calmed and she revelled in it. After a few moments she looked again at the men, and once again the fear began to move over her as it was with them. She quickly looked back to the Savior. Peace again flooded her soul. She felt Jesus looking at her as He awoke and heard His silent words in her heart. *The only way of survival in the storm of life is to keep your eyes on Hope manifest.*

At that same moment, several of the disciples came to Him. "We need help. The boat is about to sink!" They cried out to Him.

Jesus looked at the men. They were wet from the storm, and sweating from the fear. As He looked from one man to the next, compassion welled up and he stood to his feet.

"Stop!" He spoke aloud to the wind and the waves. Just as suddenly, as sudden as the peace that came to Susan the moment she looked to Him, the storm ceased. The men were caught in the middle of their screams for help. As they stopped and took in what had happened, then they stood back and looked at Him as if He were some sort of ghost.

Shaken and white with fear, one of them spoke up. "Who are you?"

The Master looked at each of them closely, eye piercing looks, even Susan felt His look and His question deeply piercing her heart. It was as if it was aimed at any and all who would follow Him.

"Where is your faith?" The words were spoken with authority and power. As they were spoken, she could not help but search her own heart, even as each man in the boat seemed to be doing.

It did not seem that He was angry with them, no, it was more like a challenge to believe. To grasp in their being what was known to be impossible and yet attainable through Him. He was offering them each, Susan included, and everyone who would choose to believe, the ability to partake of the heavenly authority which He Himself possessed.

Susan sat down in the boat and pondered deeply. She could not help but take this to heart. He wanted her to have faith. She wanted to please Him. "Yes Lord, increase my faith," she cried out in her heart.

A short while later the boat reached the other side of the lake and they all got out. Susan looked about at the desolate place that they found themselves in. She could sense an evil air about the place that made her skin shiver. Then, even as the Master came forth from the boat, a naked man came running up to them. Susan felt the presence of the evil in the air increase with the coming of the man. He was dirty and torn. His flesh was covered with wounds and scars. His hair was thick and matted and the stench of his flesh was almost unbearable. The man's eyes were full of pain and darkness. He reminded her of some sort of hopeless prisoner. Yet, as she looked closer, she saw the same hopelessness of the leper that she had seen in the heavenly courtroom. *He is no different from me without the love of the Master. Jesus is his only hope.* Susan thought to herself.

The demoniac came and fell before the Master. "What am I to you? You are Jesus, the Son of God Himself." The hideous scream of a multitude of tormenting demons came forth out of the mouth of the man. It seemed to Susan. that the demons were somehow challenging Jesus to harm the man that they were hiding in. Then the voice cried out again, this time different, as if the man himself were crying out against the strong evil presence that inhabited his being.

"I cry out to You for mercy! Do not torment me!" The man seemed momentarily lucid.

Susan saw and felt the cry of the man. It was the echo of the leper from her earlier experience, and she knew that the cry had continued throughout all time until now, and yet cried even further. It was the cry of all humanity. "Help us Master! We have no hope outside of You. Our dwelling will be with the evil horde of the darkness unless You come in Your mighty power and save us. There is no other hope! The judgment against all flesh from the first man until now remains."

She felt hot tears come down her cheeks as she made her way over to the demoniac and joined herself to his plight. *I too am in need of deliverance my Lord. I and all my brethren.*

"What is your name?" Jesus spoke, not to the man, but to the demon horde that controlled the man. In His speaking all authority was evident.

The horde spoke, betraying the defeat that they knew was theirs. "We are legion, for we are many. Do not send us into the outer darkness. Please send us out into the herd of swine over on the hillside."

The Master simply nodded and it was so. The evil horde flew off into the herd of pigs and ran violently away. The man fell to the ground as his chains of darkness were unbound and the light of God began to penetrate his being. The man was like an innocent child who had been lost and then found by his parents. He cried and clung to the hem of Jesus' garment. The disciples quickly found a robe and some wet rags to clean and dress the man. Susan could only stand and weep at the demonstration of love that was being shown.

That this man, who was so full of evil and sin, could be so easily forgiven, she felt awed. Not once did the Master condemn or even mention the sin that this demon possessed man had indulged himself in. It was so much like the parable of the prodigal son that Jesus had taught. This man, like all of the fallen humanity did not receive what he deserved, for the Master had reserved the price for sin to Himself. Susan knew that it had to be paid. Here was the Son of God paying the price and bringing undeserved freedom to man.

Even as she thought of these things, the angel appeared to her and nodded that it was time to move on. She followed and could not help but look back at the scene of love in action. The man who deserved death, and the Man who would give His own life in exchange.

Chapter Twenty-Five

Paul blinked twice. Here was his own angel, Taralah, and a new angel whom he had not met before. They both stood in front of him as he shielded his eyes from the brightness of this new angel.

Taralah spoke first. "This is Putiel. His name means God enlightens, that is why it is so bright around him. Let me touch your eyes so that it won't hurt you to see him." Taralah came toward Paul and touched him gently on the eyes.

Paul felt the feathery touch of the angel. It reminded him of a soft breeze floating across his face, yet he also felt his heart quicken to the touch as if his spirit was responding also. When the angel lifted his hand, Paul felt as though he had been washed like a dirty windshield on a muddy car. It was as if everything was clean and clear. Even the angel Taralah seemed somehow different, as though when he saw him before it was through a dark glass. Now he was able to see detail. He looked more closely at the angels, taking in the sight of them fully.

Taralah was strong. He was like a big, muscle man. He was bigger than any other man Paul had ever seen before.

In addition he seemed to vibrate with power, almost like a power transformer. When Paul came closer to the angel, he could feel the power like an electrical surge. He remembered that the angels' name meant "Power of God," and so it made sense to him that he would exude power. Taralah was dark skinned, like a man of Mediterranean descent, his hair was black and wavy, his eyes were golden brown. He wore a garment that reminded Paul of a toga, it was golden yellow and glowed with unnatural light, as if the fabric was alive somehow.

Putiel was different. He was smaller than Taralah for starters. He reminded Paul of some wise old man, someone who a person would want to ask questions of. His hands were soft and Paul had the urge to touch them. As he thought of this, the angel nodded and spoke into his mind that it would be okay to touch them.

Paul reached out slowly, touching the tips of the angels fingers gently. At first it made him feel as if he could see the love and wisdom that seemed to come from the angel. This made him want to grasp the hand as if in a handshake. When Paul did so, he felt himself begin to cry as a memory of his own father came to mind. He remembered a time when he wanted to follow his dad's advice, but had succumbed to peer pressure instead. When he had repented, his father had taken his hand and said that he was proud of him for seeing the folly of his ways. Paul had felt as if he was finally maturing and becoming wiser in his misdirected youth.

As he let go of the angel's hand, he felt awed at the light and wisdom that seemed to surge through his being.

Then the angel spoke. "The Father created us to minister His love and truth to all the saints. Most of the time when we are ministering to you, you are unaware of it. The memory that you just had was during a time when ministering angels were with you to keep you on the path of life.

The peer pressure that you were feeling was drawing you away, but the Father was pleased when you repented of your folly. He granted you more wisdom at that moment."

"We have come to bring news of a great outpouring that is about to happen in this city. You are to join a man who goes by the name of David Masterson. He is living at Riverside Park among the homeless people. It is time for the demonstration of power to manifest upon the earth. The Master told you of this before." Taralah spoke with enthusiasm. "We have waited for this time to come, and now it is upon us. This is David's angel." Taralah gestured toward Putiel. "He has brought wisdom and understanding to David, and it is time to join this light with the power of the Holy Spirit. We will join you in this venture. There will persecution at the same time. You must always remember to walk with your soul toward the heavens and not among the darkness of the earth. The enemy is very clever, as you have seen. It was very wise to see this trap of bitterness. It is the wisdom of God that has shown this to you. Keep your heart pure as you pursue the lost people with the love of the Father. We will be with you to keep you safe as the Spirit directs us. Go tomorrow and you will meet this man. Tell David that the Lord has heard his prayer for the demonstration of power to be manifest among the people, and that you have been sent to work alongside. Take your wife and daughters for they too will minister with you." Taralah finished this statement by again touching Paul on the forehead. As he did, Paul began to laugh heartily as though he would erupt. The joy that was being released over him was beyond comprehension.

As Paul continued to laugh, the angels laughed also, then they were suddenly invisible to him. At the same time Janna walked into the room.

"Are you okay? I heard you laughing and I had to come and see what was going on." Janna gazed curiously at Paul.

Paul could not stop laughing for the life of him, so he simply reached out and touched Janna on the forehead the same way that he had been touched.

Janna fell to her knees and started laughing so hard that Paul thought she would burst. They both rolled on the floor for an hour, not knowing what was so funny, yet unable to stop. Then they were joined by their two curious children who had been awakened by the noise. Paul again put his had to their foreheads, as he had with Janna, and the girls joined them in the crazy laughter that somehow seemed to liberate them from all fear. For another hour they all laughed together, the girls thought it was great since young girls of their ages are so prone to laughter anyhow, and Paul and Janna revelled in the joy that was theirs from a heavenly source.

Chapter Twenty-Six

Adaiah flew into the recesses of time with Susan under his wing. As he drew nearer the time of the crucifixion of Christ, the angel became more somber. Susan sensed that this would be the hardest part of her journey.

"How is it that we are able to travel in time like this? And why don't they see us? How are we invisible to them?" She asked the angel as they flew among what seemed like stars.

"Remember that it is spoken of Christ, 'He is the same yesterday, and today and always'. In Him all things exist, there is no time in the eternal. Many times when the saints read the Ancient book, He takes them in the Spirit to the places they are reading about. The passages seem to be real to them and indeed they are. With Him all things are possible, even the impossible. As far as being invisible to these people we are among now, we must be, or else our presence would change the writings of the Ancient book, and He has commanded that no additions be made to the words. We are here to learn from what has been taught, not add to it." Adaiah replied.

Susan thought for a moment on his response. "Do many people take this journey that I am on?"

"Yes, but each of the saints is unique and created individually. Your experience in life will never match another's. Each man and woman is assigned an angel that coincides with the type of ministry of calling upon their life. I am known as Adaiah, which means 'Yahweh has adorned.' You are to be adorned with His presence. People will be drawn to you because they will sense the presence of God upon you. This is happening even now as we travel together. The veil of communication being lifted off of you. The clearness with which you see the truth are all gifts of the ministry for which you have been called. You are no greater than your brethren, nor are you lessor. The gifts are given freely, just as His mercy is freely given. You must remember that to whom much is given, much will be required. Never compare yourself with others. It is a trap of the enemy to do so. It will only lead to pride and destruction. Always keep your eyes on the Master as you were shown in the boat. Whether or not it is stormy, keep your focus on Him and you will never be lost." Adaiah taught Susan as they flew along.

"Now we are here and it is time for the hardest part of the lesson. No matter what happens, remember that He will never leave you nor forsake you. Though you will not see me until it is over, I will be with you. No one will know of your presence as it has been all along, so you can feel free to travel among the people where they go." Adaiah looked at Susan in the eyes. "I cannot experience this as fully as you must. You are who He is dying for. I am created to minister of His goodness, but I am not in need of sanctification as you are. Do you understand?" The angel looked deeply into Susan's eyes as if somehow giving her confidence to go alone from this point.

Susan took a deep breath and inhaled the confidence she felt surrounding her. "I will be okay."

Gently the angel set her down. She looked around and saw a large gathering of people just outside the gates of a city. She turned to say good-bye to the angel, but saw that he was no longer within her vision. At first she felt strange, out of place, then panic started to take over her thoughts. Then she remembered the words that the angel had spoken about never being left alone.

"Okay Lord, I know you are with me. It's just hard to be here and yet unseen as if I'm some sort of ghost or something. Help me to trust You." Susan prayed aloud.

She began to walk toward the city. She could hear the people talking, she understood their conversation even though it was an unknown tongue to her. They spoke of a trial and how the chief priests felt that Jesus of Nazareth was some sort of false prophet. One man spoke that it would be better to do away with such as him than to have another uprising that cost more sons and daughters to be lost to the Roman soldiers. "If he was a trouble maker then he deserved to die."

Susan could see the demonic horde settled upon all the people as if this was their triumphal day. She could see and feel the confusion spread over the people like some thick cloud, obscuring their thoughts, hiding the truth from them.

As she continued on, she came to the place where they were holding Jesus prisoner. He was being whipped and beaten. She would not have known Him if it were not for the eyes. All else about Him was beyond recognition, so badly had they torn His flesh. She looked at the other prisoners and they were not near as wounded as He was. She knew their crime was murder. He was only charged with blasphemy and yet He was treated so much worse.

She walked closer toward Him and sat down on the ground by Him. It hurt to see Him so torn, and yet there was something different about Him that she had not noticed before. He was somehow familiar to her in a strange way. As she watched, she began to see and feel what it was. He was like a mirror to her soul. At first she saw the poor, pitiful leper from the celestial courtroom. He had taken the disease, the sin, the entire form of the man upon himself. Then, as she looked closer, she began to see something that made her stand and tremble. She bit her lip to stifle the scream that she felt coming up in her throat.

"It's me! I see myself, my sin. I am there with all my filth and He is wearing it." She wanted to run up to Him and take it back at first. How could she let this innocent man take her evil, her sin upon Himself? She saw not only the things she did out of ignorance, but the things she had done out of rebellion and want. Pure selfish motive, with no excuse for what she had chosen. He had taken upon Himself all the things she had done wrongly while knowing it was wrong. This made her afraid. She saw it all, every good motive, every bad one. It was all sin. The disease of it was everything she had to offer in life. There was no part of her that was uncontaminated. It hurt to see the truth.

She found herself backing away, stumbling as she hurried to get away. She ran hard and fast, breath heaving, chest pounding. At first she headed down a street, then toward a dark doorway and into an empty room. She had to hide from it, from Him. She could never bear all that she was. As she ran, she suddenly knew why the men were beating Him so furiously, for she also wanted to hit the thing He had become. They hated what they saw, for it was themselves!

Finally she found herself alone, in a dark room, in a corner. "There must be some place to hide from Him," she cried aloud. The room was deserted as if someone had left years before. It was dirty and mold grew up the walls, the smell was musty and thick. She huddled herself into the corner, trying not to think, wanting to escape the reality that had just confronted her.

Then she heard a sound. It was muffled at first, then became louder. There was a man crying in the next room.

She stood up and followed the sound. It was Peter, one of the men who had followed Jesus. He was crying bitterly and cursing himself. He had a rope and was tying it in the fashion of a hangman's noose, and then untying it. Back and forth he went, as though tottering of the edge of some forlorn precipice. All she could do was watch. She knew how he felt.

"I understand you Peter!" She spoke aloud to his unhearing ears. "I want to join you in ending it all, but that is not going to help either. We have to find Him as the resurrected Lord." She surprised herself at the wisdom with which she spoke, as much as she wanted to run and hide, she could not, for she knew the answer. "He must pay the price. There is no other way for any of us."

She watched as Peter stared at the rope for a long time, then he tossed it aside with the thoughts of suicide and left the room without it. Susan went over and touched the rope. "This would only prolong the suffering." Then she too stood up and walked out of the room.

Chapter Twenty-Seven

David was on his way to the employment office along with several other men. It was how they survived. Each morning they would go and line up for any temporary or available work that might be available. He enjoyed the camaraderie he felt with these other men. Each day as they walked together, he learned more and more about them. The common thread of homelessness had woven them into a family of sorts. He loved these people. They were all a part of creation, God's creation for whom He gave His only Son. They were so needy for life, and hope. He saw and felt their shallow existence. Many of them had at one time or another been a promising son or daughter to some parent, or maybe a businessman with so much stress that they bottomed out on life. How could he not feel compassion toward even the least of them?

At this point he turned and looked at one whom many considered to be the 'least.' Martin was a drunk, plain and simple. He was somewhere in his early 30's and yet looked about 60, so much had the hard life of alcohol taken a toll on his appearance. He worked not to live, but for money to drink. David had tried to get to know the man. Martin was quiet about himself, only once had he ever confided anything to David.

It was a night when most were asleep and David was out under the stars praying. Martin had walked up and drunkenly asked David if he had any booze. David shook his head no, and made a place for Martin to sit beside him. For some reason the man took David up on the offer. Then he asked David why he was here and David felt led to share his prison experience with the man.

As he shared, he could see the man begin to sober up. Martin even cried at one point and shook his head. "If you only knew what I have done, you would hate me. I am worse than you and I have never been to prison. I deserve to die for my crime, and yet they would not even arrest me. It was 'accidental' death and I was pardoned. How can I ever forgive myself?" Martin cried as he stood up to leave.

"Wait! Don't go! I know of One who can help you!" David jumped up and tried to restrain the man. Martin was not listening. He ran away as hard and fast as he could to find another drink to wash away his memory.

The next day when Martin came up for the walk to the employment division, David could tell that the man was closed to any conversation between them.

I guess I'll just have to pray for you, Martin. I know Someone who can heal your broken heart, forgive your horrid sin and set you free, David thought quietly to himself.

After working hard at a construction clean up, David took his pay as usual and headed for the grocery store. It was shown to him as he prayed that the best way he could serve these people, aside from teaching them the Ancient book, was to provide food and necessities. He was amazed again, as he had been each day, at how much money he was able to make, and how much food and toiletries he was able to purchase.

When he got back to the park, a line was already formed to the place where he would set up his 'shop' and hand out food and other needed items. Today he could see that SaraJean was there and had brought some medical equipment herself. She had taken employment as a Nurse Aid in a hospital and they had begun to help her with some basic items for the poor. Bandaids and aspirin, this and that, all would be appreciated. He also saw that she had started the big soup kettle to boiling. He tried to make a big, pot of nourishing soup each day and feed any who were hungry. The children would often line up as soon as they saw him coming. He loved the little ones and always tried to have some fruit to add to their plates. They were fond of him and called him 'Uncle Dave.' Then after dinner he would sit and tell them stories from the Ancient book. They always cried out for more, then the parents would come and thank him for all his care.

That night, after all the people were settled in their own camps, David began to intercede for Martin. *What can I do to reach him, Lord? He seems so close to destroying himself. I know that you love him and want to save him, Lord. Show me what to do.* David cried out again in prayer. For some reason Martin had been on his mind continuously the whole day. David continued to intercede late into the night.

It was early. Paul was excited to move on. He was preparing to make a trip over to Riverside Park and meet a man by the name of David Masterson. He had shared his experience with Janna and the girls, and today they would go over first thing after work.

All day long, Paul prayed and thought on what it would be like. *I know that I am called to see powerful demonstrations of God's love made manifest, and I'm excited, but I don't know what to expect,* he thought as he worked. It was a hot day and the construction site that he was hired to work at was busy. He was engaged with the final touches of painting when he turned and saw one of the clean up crew walking over toward him. The man had a light about him that Paul recognized. Just as he was about to speak to the man, the foreman came up and asked Paul to run an errand. As he was walking away, the man turned and looked toward Paul and their eyes met for just an instant. It was a familiar look, *family of God no doubt*, Paul thought as he walked away.

Taralah, Paul's angel smiled as he brought the 'connection' between Paul and David. He enjoyed working on what men often called 'coincidence.' Tonight when Paul and his family arrived in the park, Paul would quickly recognize the man from the clean up crew and start his 'search' of David Masterson by asking the same if he knew where to find this man. The angel loved doing these missions for the sons of God. He also looked forward to working alongside Putiel, David's angel. To mix their anointing, and bring power and light together would be a very fulfilling work.

My joy is so full when I am able to work with these chosen one's. The Master finds such value in any who will extend even the smallest measure of faith. He is always there and waiting to fill His children with His gifts, with signs and wonders, with a love that covers a multitude of sins, especially when they are willing to lay down their lives for the sake of others. If they can only begin to see that eternal treasures are of exceeding greater worth than any treasures on the earth, they would throw their money and goods to the poor as quickly as they could and live on the bare minimum of necessity. Giving would overcome taking, and the heavens would overflow with their eternal treasures. The angel spoke silently to Paul as they walked together, one all seeing, one unaware of the other.

Chapter Twenty-Eight

S usan had wandered aimlessly throughout the streets of Jerusalem for hours. She wanted to go back and follow the Messiah, but she was unsure that she could look upon her sin again. Her heart ached at what she had done, some of the sins she had committed even since knowing her Savior.

How blind I have been, to take advantage of such a pure love as His, and yet I have blindly followed my own selfish desires time and time again. How can I ever change? Is there any hope for me? For the lost people of my generation who have no idea that God even exists? I have seen the powerless preaching and the smooth flow of words that most of my peers laugh at, and I wonder how can they really be impacted with truth. They are children raised in a generation of lawlessness and selfishness. Everything that they see is viewed through eyes that have seen mostly selfish motivation by the parents of their generation. She sighed deeply and put her hands up to her eyes, rubbing them sleepily, desiring sleep to come and steal her away from the raw emotion that tore at her heart. She found a bench and laid down upon it, closing her eyes against all that was around her, she sought escape.

After a couple of hours of tossing and waking again, remembering the sight of her naked sin revealed in Christ, she heard a commotion of people approaching. As she sat up, she could see what was going on. It was a procession of people following her Lord. He was laden down with a large beam of wood upon His shoulders. He was even more wounded than she had seen Him earlier. His flesh was so torn that in many places his bones were exposed. She shuddered inwardly. As she looked upon Him, the same disgust came upon her and she knew that these men would only be satisfied when they saw Him dead. They could not bear the sight of Him any more than she could. Then she hated herself all the more for feeling this way. She remembered reading in the Ancient book of how they crucified Him and thinking that she would have done anything to protect Him. She would never allow or agree with His torture, she could never be a part of it. Now she knew that she was not only a part of it, she was included in the cause of it. Her sin was very evident to herself. She saw it there upon His shoulders and she could not deny it. Her sin was part of the burden that He carried on His back, her sin was there in His condemnation and in His death, it never left her vision. She was guilty. She was hopeless. Without the sacrifice of the Lamb, she was sentenced to eternal flame of hell and she knew it.

As He came closer to passing by where she sat, she looked up and into His eyes. She gasped her breath and let forth a deep sob as she saw the mercy He held for her, the compassion for all who so hated Him. She fell to the ground and shuddered in the dirt.

A deep dark haze began to envelop her being, swirling around her. It was as if a whirlwind had come just then, with dark, menacing black smoke it enveloped her. She knew it was unearthly, and yet she could not resist it. She felt the deserved judgment come upon her for her sin. As she began to sink into the mire of it, she knew that eternal darkness was separating her from life, from all hope. She was going to hell and she could not resist. It was her just due. It was where she belonged and she could not deny it.

Down into the recesses of darkness she sank, away from the earth and down into hell. As she travelled into the abyss, she felt the existence of her flesh disintegrate. Light was no more. She realized that in the darkest night on earth, there was always light. Light was in the blackest colors known. There was no darkness on earth like this darkness about her. She could not feel light or hope. It was empty, so devoid of any warmth, any good. It tore her soul apart like a wild animal tearing at some helpless fallen creature. She entered into a pain that she had only felt a small portion of while on the earth, the pain of loneliness. Here it was everything. She cried out to somehow cease her existence.

"Let me be no more!" Susan cried out with all of her might. "Oh that I had never been birthed. That I could somehow undo all the life that I have lived. Let me be no more!" She cried again.

Time had ceased to exist. She was eternally separated. Eons had passed, or minutes had passed, this she knew not. He existence was part of the darkness. She felt the clawing demons surrounding her, the cursing and wailing of a million other lost souls with whom she could not communicate and yet with whom she dwelled. Isolation and separation. Pain and fear. Darkness consuming over and over again, sinking forever into a black drowning from which she knew no escape. She had no control. She hurled against the eternal existence of hell.

"No way out. No way out." The demons screamed. "The sin of man has separated you forever." They seemed to relish her demise. "You will feed our hunger. We will consume you forever. Our bread is in your fall. Ha ha ha." They shrieked aloud.

She felt the pull of sharp teeth tearing at her soul. Pain. How she wanted to pass out. To find some relief from her misery. "Help me! Help me Jesus!" She cried out in desperation.

The cross was put into the ground and Jesus hung upon it. Upon His shoulders all sin ever committed funnelled down to Him. All evil was loosed upon Him. He was like a magnet for every horrible thing done. Utter blackness came over Him. He felt the complete separation of light from darkness.

"My God, why have you forsaken me?" The cry came forth from His tortured lips. He was complete with sin. All deity was removed as the judgment came forth over Him. He saw the angels with their backs turned at the command of the Father. He searched the heavens for the familiar. He was man. He carried every burden, every weight, every cancer, every murder. It poured over and over him as He took His last breaths.

As the last bits of sin and disease filtered down over Him, He looked around. He saw the leering faces, the mocking crowd. He saw their hate. He was so full of their hate that no man could ever know the weight of His burden. He summoned faith. His hope was so fully in what was not seen, what was not felt. He cried out with it, "Father, forgive them! They don't know what they are doing." He sighed His last breath. Darkness enveloped Him. A last whisper came forth from His dying lips. "Into Thy hands I commit My spirit." He died.

Chapter Twenty-Nine

Paul and his family had just arrived at the Park. He looked around nervously and wondered how he would ever find this man who he had never met and never seen. He closed his eyes and prayed. *Lord, how do I find him? Where do I look?* He silently petitioned the heavens.

Go over to the drinking fountain on the west side of the park, came the still small voice of the Spirit. Paul sighed and wondered if this was his mind speaking or if he had heard correctly. He started over to the fountain by faith.

"It is so hard to go by faith, isn't it Janna?" He turned and spoke to his wife as he led the way.

Janna was taking in all the sights around her. "I cannot believe how many people are living here! Why haven't we come here before? Look at all the needs, all the children, all the people," she pointed to different families as they walked. "I have been too sheltered, Paul. I have asked the Lord what I could do each day and yet I never thought of coming here." She touched Paul's arm and sighed deeply.

"All in God's time, Janna." He responded quietly. "He knows our hearts and that we are willing. He will show us now how we can help. He has been preparing us all along, you know. What with Susan coming to us and the special way of helping her to know Him, now He is ready to give us more little lambs to feed. When you are faithful with the small things, He always brings the increase." Paul smiled at Janna warmly. He was feeling his faith well up within.

As they came close to the fountain, Paul looked around. Then he saw a group of people serving others some sort of food, or soup. Paul gazed at the young man in charge. There was something familiar about that man, he thought. Just then the man looked up and looked at Paul. It was that same man from the construction site earlier! Paul smiled. As their eyes met, a smile of welcoming came to the other man's face, and Paul walked over toward him.

"Hi, my name is Paul Chandler." He introduced himself to David. "I saw you at the construction site today and almost made it over to acquaint myself with you, but I was called away on an errand. You have a light about you that makes me wonder if you are a Christian. Are you?" Paul asked the young man boldly.

David looked Paul over and immediately liked him. "Yes, I am a follower of Jesus. I also wondered that about you today when I saw you at the job." David smiled warmly as he responded. "Are you hungry? Would you like to join us for a meal?"

Paul looked at the soup and smiled. "It really looks good, but we just ate. This is my family, my wife Janna and my two daughters, Joy and Katherine." Paul gestured toward his family as they joined him. "We are here on a mission of sorts. Maybe we could ask you a few questions when you have a moment?" Paul saw that the line for food was growing and he did not want to keep the man any longer.

"Yes, I'm almost through here, just a few minutes and I would love to talk with you." He responded heartily. "Just have a seat over there by that blue blanket on the ground," he pointed.

"Okay, we'll be here when you're done, don't hurry on account of us." Paul walked over toward the blanket. As he sat there, he took in all the sights around him, small campsites of people all over the park. He had heard of this place, this refuge for the homeless, but he had no idea that there were so many people. The jobs were scarce in the town and the rent was high. It was hard to make it these days, especially if you lost your job. He felt the despondency and hopelessness around him.

"These people have so little, Daddy," Joy spoke aloud. "How come they are living here and not in houses like we do?" She looked inquisitively at her father.

"Honey, there are a lot of hard things that happen to people. That is why we always give thanks for what we have, that we have a roof over our heads and food to eat. Some people have so little, that is why we try and share what we do have. God provides for us and he wants us to help provide for others." Paul spoke gently to his eldest daughter. She was always so sensitive to her surroundings.

"Why can't people who have a lot of money share with these people? Maybe we should tell them that there are hungry people who need their help down here and they could give some of their stuff away. I can share my blankets and some of my clothes too. I don't always eat everything that mom gives me either, maybe I could bring it here and share it with those kids over there." She pointed her finger at some small children playing close by.

Paul smiled and sighed. "I think that would be wonderful. You need to ask your mother what you should bring to share and she will help you bring things that can really help. As far as people who have a lot of money helping, well not everyone can see others in need the way you do. Many people have their security in their possessions and their money, and cannot part with it. We must pray for them to have Jesus in their hearts and then they could share because their belongings wouldn't be their satisfaction anymore." Paul explained.

Joy looked seriously at her father. "I know what you mean Daddy. Sometimes I want to be selfish with my toys because I feel that they are very important to me. Then I get mad at my sister when she yells because I won't share. I'm sorry, daddy. I'm going to pray really hard that Jesus will come in my heart and that I could be mostly satisfied with Him instead of my toys." The youngster spoke resolutely.

At that moment David walked up and joined them. "So, are you new campers here? How can I help you?" He spoke cheerily.

Paul looked at David and answered. "We have been sent here to find a man by the name of David Masterson. Would you know how we could contact him, or do you know of him?"

David felt the color leave his face. He thought to himself, *No one knows I'm here, what do these people want?* He looked at Paul somberly. "Yes, I know David. What do you want with him?" He spoke guardedly.

Paul saw the change in the man's appearance and felt his apprehension. "We are here by divine order. The Lord spoke to me that David has been praying for help to come his way in the ministry that is going on here, and we have been sent by God to help. Specifically I was told that He has prayed for a demonstration of power to be manifest among the people, and we have been sent in answer to his prayer." Paul spoke with a boldness that was unusual to himself.

David felt himself relax. He stared at the family and wondered at the divine intervention that was being made into his life. He was amazed at how God works. He smiled at Paul and spoke, "I am David Masterson!"

Chapter Thirty

The storm clouds gathered on the earth as Jesus Christ was pulled down toward the abyss. Into the darkness, the prison of the damned, He descended. The earth began to quake in fear of its very creator sinking into its midst. Like an atom finding fission within itself, the earth shook and rebelled at the content of its inward part. He was not digestible. He was the One who formed the earth, how could He ever be consumed by hell. It would never be so. The entire abyss shook and vibrated violently. Wave upon wave of tremors and violence struck the eternal regions of damnation. He was pure light amid the blackest darkness. As Jesus descended He became stronger and stronger, death could not hold Him, darkness could not devour Him. He became like a huge muscle man, full of strength, power and righteousness. His countenance shown with majesty and determination, He was the conqueror, and He had done what was necessary to gain access into the regions of darkness. He outsmarted the enemy, who thought that killing Jesus would bring sure victory. Once the blood payment had been met, then victory and resurrection power invaded. Truth reigned. He came for the keys, and to free the prisoner who put his trust in God.

The demons screamed in agony as the light blinded their dark eyes. They could not understand what had happened to their secure domain, what Presence was this? Where was the victory they knew moments earlier as they had heaped insult upon insult as Jesus suffered the cross? Something unheard of had interrupted their party, something that would eventually end their existence in an eternal flame of fire. Still further into the abyss He penetrated. Downward to the very core of all evil existence.

The fallen angel Lucifer awaited in terror, for he held keys in his hands that had been his from the very beginning of man's fall. The keys of death and Hades, the keys of eternal damnation for all creation doomed by the judgment of fallen man.

Lucifer shook and feared. His beauty was fading and as the Conqueror approached he could feel all his authority melt away. His once beautiful color, his lovely personage, all of it was fading. He was becoming as ugly as the sin for which he had so long held rule over. He was the master of the eternal. He was on his throne and now One who was greater was coming to take away his authority. He had lost the battle. He had to surrender.

Jesus Christ entered the demonic throne room, as the walls of the chamber heaved and sighed with His presence. How could someone so pure and righteous be in this horrid place? The earth trembled violently, as if trying to stop the invasion of truth. Lucifer tried to hold his position at his throne, his sharp nails digging into the fabric of the chair, but darkness can never stand in the midst of light. At the entrance of Jesus Christ he flung himself to his knees before the Lord of Glory. Cowering, shivering in the exposed nature of his evil, trying to maintain his sense of pride, yet knowing His creator was even now taking back all the glory this fallen angel had once known. Satan watched as the glory fled him, falling away like a garment that was never really his in the first place, it returned to the One who truly owned it. He shivered again as the beauty he had once known left him exposed to the truth of what he really was, empty, ugly, naked and filthy. He shuddered as he saw this, his eyes sinking farther into the empty, dark sockets that held no light, no hope. Evil spirits came forth from him: lust, greed, hatred, perversion, filth, each one bowing low before the King. One last spirit came forth, refusing to bow. The spirit of blasphemy. It stood in defiance against the Lord and against the Holy Spirit that empowered this event, and it was then proclaimed that this would be the unforgivable sin as that spirit stood there. No one would blaspheme against the Holy Spirit and survive, for this spirit was cursed more than any other. This spirit was the cause of Satan's own demise, and for this he would never, never return to glory, but would burn forever in the fiery pit.

The devil reached his hand up surrendering the keys. It was over. Lucifer bowed his face low to the dirt in homage to One greater and admitted his utter defeat.

Susan felt the tremors of the abyss, she felt the demons shudder. Remembering the words of the angel, that she would never be forsaken, faith welled up again.

"Jesus, Lord Jesus save me!" She cried out again to the darkness. Shafts of light began to filter through, as truth erupted into the darkness surrounding her. Hope welled up in her heart causing a song to burst forth from her lips. "Amazing Grace how sweet the sound!"

As the light penetrated her, she felt and saw the form return to her being. Again she thought of how all existence was in Him. "In Him we live and move and have our being," she rejoiced aloud as she was being carried upward, upward. She could see Him and feel Him all around her. He brought salvation, and He carried her out of the abyss, out of the eternal damnation that was a just and deserved payment for her sin. Jesus Christ had overcome all the evil, all the disease. She saw the keys in His hands and she cried. The keys had written on them the judgements of man, from the fall and onward. One said Hades, and another said Death. They were keys that had controlled the outcome of each life lived on the earth. They had fallen into the wrong hands when Adam and Eve first sinned. The Devil had used those keys as his power to torment both the living and the dead. Now the keys belonged to God, now they would bring freedom to all who would receive the sacrifice of the Lamb.

Up out of the abyss and past the regions of the damned she was carried. She felt as if a knight on a white horse had come to rescue her. Then as she looked around she began to realize that she had been brought out of the abyss and was once again seated in the heavenly courtroom. She looked and saw the little lamb who had eaten the judgment scroll, it now lay on the altar dead.

"Let the man go free!" Came the voice of the Judge. "The lamb has taken his place. He has brought the payment with Him in the form of His blood." The Judge pointed to the sacrificial altar and there on top of it was the blood of the Lamb, but the little lamb was no longer slain. It had stood up, and was alive and moving about.

Then He came into the room. It was Jesus Christ. He was pure and spotless, bright and powerful. He came with the keys attached to the belt of His garment. He put His hand on the leper and the leper became clean. The man stood and cried as he saw that he was healed. Then he bowed and kissed the feet of Jesus. At the same moment all the celestial inhabitants came and bowed. Susan joined. All creation bowed at the feet of the Son. The twenty-four elders took the crowns off their heads and laid them at His feet as they too bowed, and sang glorious praises.

"He is worthy of all praise and honor and glory for now and ever more." Susan cried aloud as she realized what a beautiful gift of life was so freely given to her.

Adaiah was next to her as she bowed. The angel looked lovingly at Susan. "Now you are ready to share in the testimony of the Lamb. Go and tell all who will listen of the price that was paid and the salvation that was wrought for them. There is no need for any to perish. From the greatest to the least of all mankind He has paid the price. You know what the price was, and you know what He has given them." The angel spoke to his charge and watched as she stood boldly and began a proclamation of her faith.

"I receive all that has been given for me. I see that nothing I can ever do, or accomplish can pay the price for my sin. All is in my Lord Jesus and I stand fully covered by His sacrifice." She turned and faced the Lamb of God.

"Inhabit me with Your glorious Spirit and I will be a vessel of Your praise and honor. Send me forth only as a vessel filled with Your words and Your power and I will go among the nations. My life is forever in Your hands my Lord, and I am forever Your handmaiden. Thank You for Your blood, for the daring rescue from Hades, and for Your light which ever lights my path. Now I know that nothing can ever separate me from Your love. I am safe with You, Master."

Susan spoke forth of her love to the One on the throne, and to the Son.

Jesus spoke. "I am coming soon! You must tell them all. It is time for My marriage and I have waited for you. You and your brothers and sisters are to be My bride. Look and see that the table is now being set for the banquet feast at the Marriage supper of the Lamb."

Then He turned and gestured with His hand, and there before her appeared a vast hall with an endless table wonderfully prepared with a feast. The table was beautiful with golden dishes, and large vases of extraordinary flowers, hues of purple and magenta, yellows and blues. All the colors of the rainbow were there, glowing and pulsing with life.

A host of angels stood there awaiting to serve the many who would soon come and dine.

"There are many who are yet to be invited. Do not waste any time. The call is even now going forth and the time on earth is short. Tell them, Susan. Tell them of My love, how I long for them. I would die over and over if it meant that I could bring them close to Me. Yet I have paid the price. There is nothing that separates them from My love accept that which I cannot and will not control. To each is given a will and they must choose Me freely. Each person makes a choice and you must tell them of the choice. I give you My Spirit freely to empower you for your mission. Go now, tell them of my Love." Jesus came to Susan at this point and touched her on the forehead. "You are sealed with My love and the Holy Spirit."

"Yes, Lord, I will!" Susan cried out. The light began to fade as she tried to keep the vision of Christ in her mind. She felt as if she were falling. The heavenly scene from which she was a part was disappearing and she was falling as if to the earth. Adaiah was there flying beside her, holding her up.

"I will be here with you. I am assigned to help you but you will no longer see me. Have faith, child. Believe in that which you cannot see. Know that you are never alone. Do not allow the cares of the world to come in and steal what you have been given here, hold onto this vision and let it come forth in you for the sake of the lost." Adaiah spoke tenderly as a father would speak to his daughter.

Susan felt the love and caring that the angel had for her. "Don't worry. I'm okay now. I have been to the abyss and been rescued by my Savior. How can anything be worse than that? The only hard part will be my longing to return to the heavens and worship Him forever."

Now even the angel was fading and Susan felt herself become heavy with sleep. Back into her body she went, her journey was completed.

Chapter Thirty-One

Paul and David spoke late into the night as they sat around a camp fire at the park. As they each shared their recent past, they seemed to find a bond that they knew was special. God had brought them together and they were in awe of Him for doing so. Janna and the girls were introduced to SaraJean and began to help her with clean up of the little soup kitchen. They all enjoyed one another in their new found friendship.

"How can we begin to make an impact upon these people for the sake of our Lord Jesus?" Paul asked David sincerely. "I want you to know that I am here for you. I want to fully commit my time and efforts to you. My home is also open to you and any whom you bring along. We don't have a lot of space, but we will use what is there." Paul looked tenderly at his new found friend. He so wanted to burst with excitement at finally being called to serve the Lord.

"I appreciate that, Paul." David replied. "I am still in awe that you are here. I believe that we should begin by praying together as often as possible and seeking what the Father is doing here. Jesus only did what the Father was doing and I want to be sure and keep the priorities right with Him.

There are many poor here, and we must find God's path in helping them or we will lose our focus and become frustrated by the pressing need about us. I have learned this while I have been staying here. Sometimes it is important to allow a person to come to the end of their rope before extending the lifeline or else they might not be fully ready to receive the One who can give them true life. To rescue them from their trials before the right time could only send them hurling toward damnation. We must always look beyond the surface of human suffering and see the soul. I am not interested in rescuing their bodies from daily life and its trials, I want to see eternal fruit brought forth here." David spoke clearly and confidently.

Paul was amazed at the wisdom that the young man spoke. It reminded him of the angel 'Putiel,' David's angel. The same wisdom was flowing from the young man that Paul had felt when he had touched the hand of the angel. Silently he thought, *I wonder what David would think if I told him about meeting his angel the other night.* Paul wasn't sure how much he should share with the man.

David continued as Paul listened. "I believe in the power of God, Paul. When I read in the Ancient book of how Jesus Christ ministered to the people, and how He called us to do even greater works because He was going to His Father, how can I doubt. I know that the greater works are not in evidence around me, or else there would be signs of it. I have not felt led to join any of the local Churches around here yet even though I have prayed for direction. I have been in prison for a long time and before that I had never been to a Church. Yet in my heart I know that I am part of the Church, a building not made with hands, and you and I are here together having Church. The Ancient book teaches that where two or more are gathered in His name, He is in their midst."

David sighed. "I'm sorry if I am talking too much. It's just that I have so much bottled up inside me and I have so longed for someone to speak with who would understand. These people around me here are so fragile. I must use so much caution to lead them to the Living waters." He stopped and looked tenderly at Paul. "Thank you for coming, my friend."

Paul felt his heart surge with love and a kindred spirit. He thought of a portion of the Ancient book where a man named David had a friend named Jonathan. They too were close, it was ordained by God. "I'm truly looking forward to our relationship in the Lord, David. I know that God is doing something wonderful here."

At that moment Janna and the girls came up and joined them. "I'm sorry to have to break up your conversation, but I have two sleepy little girls here. Could we invite David to come over and pray with us at the house while I put the girls to bed and check on Susan?"

Paul and David stood up. "Would you consider coming to our house tonight David?"

David bowed his head for a moment to check with his Lord. Paul and Janna did the same. After a moments silence he looked up and spoke. "For some reason I am not free to join you tonight. I must stay here and intercede for one of the men who has been on my heart very strongly. His name is Martin and I covet your prayers for him. Can you come again tomorrow?"

Paul nodded his head and asked if they could all join hands and pray before they left. As they did, he petitioned the heavens for the sake of Martin, and for some reason added that God might spare his life. Paul knew nothing of this Martin fellow, but the prayer felt right and so he had prayed it.

After they arrived home, Janna went in to check upon Susan. Excitedly she came out and called for Paul to join her. Quickly he came and joined her in the room which Susan had occupied for the past few weeks.

"Look at her Paul. Something is different. She looks like she is sleeping normally. Maybe she is about to wake up." Janna spoke, thrilled at the possibility.

Just then Susan began to stir. Slowly she opened her eyes and rubbed them. "What is going on? Where am I? Where did the angel go?" She sat up in the bed and looked around.

"It's okay Susan. We are here." Replied Janna. "You have been in another place for some time now. Kind of like the Wizard of Oz or something. But you're back now and we have missed you so much. Would you like to sleep until morning? It's late at night now. Or do you want to get up?"

"I'm really hungry?" Susan's voice cracked as she spoke. "Do you think I could have something to eat? How long have I been asleep? Do you mind terribly if I get up now?" Susan felt tired and weak, yet excited about all that had happened to her. "I'm back!" She spoke as she stood up. "Whoa!" She started to fall back on the bed. "I guess I stood up to fast. I feel so weak." Susan paled as she sat down.

"Here let us help you! Once you get some solid food into you it will be okay." Paul spoke as he offered her assistance with Janna at her other side.

As they walked into the kitchen, Susan blinked hard at the bright light. "Boy, I feel as if I've been asleep for weeks or something. How long has it been?" She asked weakly.

"Pretty close to a month." Paul replied. "We have had to feed you baby food since you could not be awakened to eat normally. An angel came to us and told us that you were okay, that is why we didn't take you to the hospital. But let me tell you, it has been a faith walk to know that you weren't sick or something. Occasionally you would speak out some words about where you were and we would relax and trust the Lord that He had you in His care." Paul smiled tenderly and touched Susan on the head like he did his own daughters. "Welcome back, child."

Susan smiled as she sat gingerly at the kitchen table, fingering the red and white checkered tablecloth. "You won't believe where I've been. I do agree with you though, God had me in His care in more ways that I can tell you." Susan remembered her recent excursion to hell. "He has never let me out of His sight, that I know for sure."

Then Janna came from the kitchen with a plate full of cold chicken and potato salad, some milk and bread. As she set the plate before Susan, the girls' eyes opened wide and she smiled a huge grin. "Here ya go sweetheart, eat up now. We can wait until later to hear of all your journey. Now you must eat and be revived." Susan didn't answer as her mouth was too busy enjoying the wonderful food.

Chapter Thirty-Two

The sun was bright in the early morning as David sat upon the picnic bench reading from the Ancient book. There had been no work available for that day, so he had come back to the park to study. He could not help but let his mind wander a bit though He thought of the meeting the night before, and his new found friend, Paul. God was so good to him, he smiled to himself as he thought. He did not hear the footsteps that approached.

"David, you must come quick!" SaraJean was there looking totally in a fright. "It's Martin. He has been found all in a heap. I think something is terribly wrong with him. David, I'm scared for him!" She sobbed as she spoke.

David jumped up and asked. "Where is he, SaraJean? Quick, take me to him." He followed as she turned to lead.

As they ran across the park, David prayed that Martin would still be alive. "Please God, don't let him die without knowing you. Save him from hell Lord, have mercy on his soul!" He cried out as he ran.

As they approached, there was a small crowd of people gathering. David came up breathlessly. He bent down on one knee at Martin's side and spoke close to his ear.

"Martin! Martin! Can you hear me? It's David." He felt
for the man's heartbeat. Yes, he was alive. There was no
response though. David tried to open the man's eye. The
pupil was fixed. There was no reaction to the light.

At that moment SaraJean spoke. "David, I saw him
yesterday. He was so drunk, I've never seen him so intoxi-
cated and able to stand. He had gotten some money from
someone and he was drinking really hard stuff. I think he is
in an alcoholic coma. Someone has already gone to summon
help. They should be arriving soon." She took a deep breath
to try and calm herself. "He can't die without Jesus, David.
I've been praying hard that God would save him."

David stood up and took off his coat to put under
Martin's head. "God has kept him alive so far. Don't give
up, SaraJean. Just keep on believing." He kneeled over the
stricken man once again.

Just then one of the onlookers spoke. "Look at you
people! Why are you so concerned? He was just a useless
drunk. I say he is better off dead. He wanted to die, now let
him go. He went the way he wanted to, drunk. If you ask
me, that is the best way to go, just stay drunk and happy!
Besides he was just taking up space. What with all the problems around here and this park, it's better this way." The
man looked at David defiantly.

Before David could respond, another onlooker spoke.
"He's right man. That guy was nothin but trash. He just gets
drunk and slobbers all over the place. Why, I even heard that
the guy was responsible for the death of some kid. I say it's
his just due. Let him die, the sooner the better." The man
looked over toward Martin and spit on the ground. He
grunted in disgust and walked away.

David stood and looked at all the others who had gathered around. "Don't you see how wrong it is to judge this
man? He is no different from any of us here. Maybe his
crime is bad, but there is not one person among us now

who has not sinned. We are all hopeless in our sin! We are all doomed without help from somewhere. Which one of you can save yourselves? Which one of you has never sinned? Come here and show me the way to eternal life if you can." He stopped and looked at them intently. Slowly he turned until he had met the eyes of each person. Silently he prayed for the convicting power of the Holy Spirit to fall on them. After a short time of heavy stillness, where the air felt like lead to many of them, one of the men spoke.

"Do you know the answer? What about you, huh! Can you save yourself from this life?" The man searched David's face, half in hope and half in mockery.

David took a deep breath. He could feel the anointing power of the Holy Spirit come upon him. Words of life began to form in his mind.

"There is One way only. There has been a door opened to life and freedom and any who will receive it can enter. God, the maker of all heaven and earth, of all mankind, wants to give this way to you. I have found the way and I can show you also. There is no other way. Do you want to know the Way?" He spoke slowly and with authority. Martin lay on the ground, the color of death marking his face, causing the crowd to take David even more seriously.

Then a woman spoke, "Tell me of this Way! I want to find something better than this!" She pointed at the comatose man on the ground. He was drooling out of one side of his mouth and his breath was gurgling as if he were drowning in his own saliva. They could each see for themselves that Martin stood at the threshold of death.

"Yes, you are right. There is a better way. His name is Jesus Christ and He is God's own son, the Messiah. He came to us and took death upon His own shoulder's so that we could receive His life when He was raised again. He overcame death, and hell and all the charges brought against man. He says to any who will come that He will receive them.

He is the Way, the Truth and the Life. He is eternal and He is here now. He not only gives eternal life, but He also gives freedom from sin here and now. He can free you from your slavery to drugs, sex and alcohol. He can heal the wounds of your abuse, of rape and incest. He can free your hearts from the bondage of bitterness that keeps you sick and gives you disease. Repent of your sins and be baptized into His Name. Receive His payment for your sin and in exchange you will get His life." David held out his hands to them. "Come and I will baptize you in His name!"

One of the men began to cry at this point. He reached out to David as if a lifeline had been thrown to a drowning man. "Help me, Sir! I have sinned and my sin is driving me hard. I dream each night of horrible things. Blackness tries to overtake me in my sleep and I wake up in a cold sweat. I have been to many Doctors and there has been no help. I have tried to drink my pain away and there is only momentary loss of memory then it all comes flooding back. Do you think this Jesus that you speak of will have me?" The man fell to David's feet in a sob.

"Yes! Come with me over to the river and I will baptize you." David turned and looked to the rest of the crowd. "If you want to come, follow me and I will show you the way to Jesus Christ." He saw that the ambulance had arrived and asked quickly which hospital they would be taking Martin to before turning away with the small crowd who had sought salvation.

Like little wounded children they followed him. They were hungry for life and he knew it. The Holy Spirit had manifested Jesus Christ to them and their faith was great. "Lord, I sure wish that You would send Paul about now, I could sure use some help with these people." He prayed silently as they walked.

Chapter Thirty-Three

Paul, Janna, and Susan sat together at the kitchen table. Susan was trying to share some of her experience, but each time she tried to tell them she would begin to cry and be unable to continue.

"I can't begin to put it into word's, so much was shown to me. I see how much we are loved by God, and how we have nothing to offer Him except our lives and our hearts. He has paid such a dear price for our salvation. I never want to take advantage of it. I know that my life here is my cross to bear now. Just as He bore the cross of this world and its suffering's, so must I. Not that I would ever begin to compare my cross with His. He has shown me that in my life there will be a cost to following Him. As I sat at His feet for many days He taught of this. We must choose to take up our cross each day. We must fight against the stronghold of the flesh and its control over us and grasp the cross and the sufferings of Christ. He showed the way for us to walk in. He told me that if I would lay down my life, then I would gain it eternally. I do not expect to find my kingdom here as many have thought. I want to be like Him, He invested all in another place, in an eternal bank where nothing can corrode.

I want to serve Him with all my heart just as He served the people. I see it as the answer to my seeking, I do not want a home here, I want to live each day for my home there. I don't know how to say it. I know that we must have homes to bring people to and feed them, I just don't want my home to be for me, I want it to be for Him." She sighed helplessly. "I hope I'm not rambling. It's just that there was so much. Where do I begin?"

Paul laughed out loud. "You're doing just fine, all in due time. God will use your experience in His own way and it will be good."

Janna smiled and added, "He is right, don't try to tell it all today. Just live it out as He shows you. Be at peace with your humanity and let God be God. He will give you the right words at the right time. Just keep your eyes on Him."

"Oh, I can't believe you said that. He told me the same thing when I was in a boat ..." Susan sighed deeply at the thought and her eyes glistened with tears. "He is so wonderful! I'm sorry! I just can't speak of it yet." She sobbed even louder.

Paul reached out toward her, putting his hand on her head. "It's okay child. Do not try so hard."

As Paul sat back he felt the pull of the Spirit in his heart, he stood up to leave. "I think I will go in and pray for a bit. Do you mind?" He turned to Janna.

Janna smiled sweetly. "No dear. Please go ahead. I just want to hog Susan to myself for a while anyway. I've missed her so much."

Paul walked down the hall toward the bedroom. He could not help but feel drawn to thinking about David. As he entered the room, he kneeled on the floor beside the bed. He began to lift David up in prayer to the Father. *Lord, you know where he is right now and I pray that You will guide his steps. Bless him with your Presence. Be a shining light in him, Lord, in the midst of the darkness.* As Paul prayed, he began to weep for the man. He felt as if he was interceding on David's behalf. "Something must be up!" He thought aloud. *Lord, you know where he is and what is happening to him right now. I pray that You will give him wisdom and guidance. Send Your angels to minister truth and strength. Help him to stand fast in the anointing that You have given him.* Paul continued to pray for his friend throughout the morning.

David was at the river with about 12 people who had followed him there. SaraJean was at his side as he spoke of the new life God was giving each of them. As he took the first man to the water to baptize him, he felt the power of the Spirit fall upon him. The man was verbally declaring his sin and desire for Jesus to come into his heart as David took the man down into the cold water. As the man came up out of the water, the Holy Spirit came upon him and he began to speak in an unknown language. He was laughing and crying and dancing about, the whole crowd seemed to gasp at him.

As this occurred, several people came up at once and wanted to be next. David had to get them to be patient. "SaraJean, will you come over and help me please? I feel that you are just as qualified to help baptize these as I am. You are also a believer." SaraJean walked over toward one of the women and taking her by the arm led her out into the water. As the woman was brought down into the water, the Holy Spirit again fell, this time on both of them, SaraJean and the woman began to sing and shout in an unknown tongue.

As David continued to baptize, over and over the same thing would happen, until it looked as if they were having some sort of drunken party. Several people from the homeless camps began to wander over and ask what was going on. One of the men was an Iranian. He was clearly shaken as he walked up to David.

"How is it that this woman over here," he pointed over at SaraJean, "can speak in my native language? It is not even a common language in my land. It is a language of my family clan and not well known." The man seemed almost indignant.

David eyed the man keenly. "What is she saying?"

The man walked closer to SaraJean and listened. As she spoke, he clutched at his heart and began to cry. He walked back to David after a short time and bowed low. "She has spoken of my secrets. How can she know these things? I have shared them with no man. What shall I do? Surely this is the power of Allah!"

David touched the man on the shoulder. "Has Allah ever spoken like this to you before? Have you ever heard of such a thing coming from a person who does not even know what they are saying? How can you say this is Allah?" He spoke with the man gently.

The man thought hard and kept his eyes to the ground. After a moment he spoke. "I have never heard of such a thing from Allah. I have rebelled against the harsh god of my land because I could not stand the heartless god and the way my people suffer. Who is it then? What God is this who can know the heart of a man and tell of all his secrets? Tell me and I will serve this God with all my heart for surely He will show me His love!" The man had fallen to the ground before David and was bowing at his feet.

"I'm a simple man! Do not bow before me, but bow before Jesus Christ, God's own Son. Let me baptize you also. Repent of your sin and ask him to be your Lord and Master. Ask Jesus to come into your heart and He will come and live with you." David led the man toward the water.

In the meantime, the crowd of people was preaching and singing and sharing of God's love with any who would listen to them. SaraJean continued to baptize as many who wanted to come and they all received wonderfully of the Holy Spirit.

After most of the day had gone by, and David saw that the crowd had grown, he turned to SaraJean and asked what food they had to offer.

"David, we have enough for maybe five people. We gave so much last night!" She looked at him apologetically. "I'm sorry."

Just then, Paul, Janna, the girls and Susan arrived. David turned and walked up with his hand out to Paul. "I prayed that you would come! You would not believe what has happened here today."

At the same moment he quickly asked SaraJean to bring the food they had. She sighed and turned to go. "I will bring it, but God will have to stretch it!" She muttered under her breath.

Paul and David stood aside as David filled him in on the details of how the day was spent. "Finally Paul," he concluded, "We must feed these people and there is very little food. And we must get to the hospital and check on Martin. I know that we must pray for him." David finished, out of breath.

Paul looked around incredulously. "Surely God has moved among you today." He spoke in wonder and awe.

As SaraJean returned with the food, and Janna busily set about getting the makeshift cookstove to working, David asked Paul to bless the food and feed them all.

Paul looked around at all the people. There must have been 50 or 75 people gathered about. He saw the meager amount of food, two loaves of bread and some leftover stew and smiled. *So this is how it will start, Huh? Okay Lord! I will be faithful and believe You for the increase.*

"Father, we come before You today in Thanksgiving for all Your abundance. Bless this food and nourish our souls as well as our bodies! Amen." Paul prayed sincerely.

He turned and walked over to Janna. "No matter what you see in the pot, just keep ladling it out. Do not make any comment on what is in there. Do you understand?" Janna smiled as the faith arose in her. "My pleasure honey!" She set about to the task of feeding the hungry. She sang wonderful songs about Jesus as she worked and hardly even looked into the pot to see what was left. It did not matter to her. "My God has enough for everyone!" Janna spoke aloud to no one in particular.

Chapter Thirty-Four

At the hospital, Martin lay in a coma. Several Doctors had come into his room and many tests had been given. Finally the prognosis was listed on his chart that he was not expected to live. One of the tests had revealed that his brain had shut down and soon his heart would also stop beating. It was just a matter of time before it was over.

Martin had never experienced such blackness. He thought he must have been asleep in a dark tunnel or something and he tried to grope around to find his way out. "There has to be a doorknob, or an opening of some sort here. Where am I anyway? Boy, I must have really tied one on last night. It was some pretty powerful stuff that I was drinking alright. I was hoping to just end it all. I just wanted to become oblivious and cease to exist. I guess I failed. I'm still here, wherever here is?"

He continued to wander around the dark aimlessly. Suddenly he felt a sharp pain in the calf of his leg. "Ouch," he cried out. He reached down to try and stop the pain, but he was unable to realize his hand. Then he tried to use his other hand and the same thing happened. Finally he reached up with what he thought was his hand and tried to feel his face, again nothing. Panic rose up in him. *Am I paralyzed or something? Is this a dream?* Just then he felt another sharp pain to his calf. This time the pain continued and Martin began to swear at it. As he swore, he felt a hot breath of some creature come close to where his face should have been.

Soon a hideous voice spoke in a menacing whisper close to his missing ear. "You are mine now!" Came a scratchy deep voice thick with hate. "I will feed off of you forever. As soon as you are completely dead I am going to pull you into my cavern and chew your disgusting soul until it rots. And if you think the pain will ever end you are mistaken. I own you. You are dying and there is no hope for you. Ha ha ha!" The demon of darkness laughed as he dove into Martin's stomach and began to tear apart his bowels.

"Help me! Someone help me!" Martin screamed out into the darkness. His thoughts were tormented by the possibility that he could be in hell. *No, it cannot be! I do not believe in hell! There has to be something else. Why is this happening?* He screamed again and again. He could not run. He could not move. He was unable to see or do anything but submit to the torturous pain that the demon was inflicting upon his pitiful existence. Somehow he continued to exist, but not in the flesh, he had no control over his body, it was an existence that he did not understand. He thought that maybe this was his soul. He had heard somewhere that the soul was forever, that it was an eternal part of his being.

"You are so stupid!" The demon smacked his lips loudly in Martin's face. "You humans are so stupid! You think that what you choose to believe is the truth. How blind and stupid you are! How can you think that you are powerful enough to believe that whatever you make up about the hereafter is the truth? Even we demons know that God is the creator of all that is. Yet you foolish humans think that because you have a mind and can think, you can choose what you want to believe and that will make it so. How easily you are deceived! Of course, I am glad that so many are deceived. Because of deception, I can feed off of you and fill my stomach on the eternal existence of your soul. There is no other way for the people of earth. All have to choose. If the payment is not paid for sin by the only One who can pay it, then you are forever sentenced to eternal damnation. There is only black and white, no middle ground. Even I had to choose. I was once an angel of great beauty. I was created to serve and love people like you. But I choose to follow someone who I thought would be the conqueror. Lucifer was magnificent and I thought he would be the greater. How I was wrong. He lost the battle from the start, and now he no longer has the keys. I am subject, along with him and all who follow in his rebellion, to dwell in this place of eternal suffering. Your rotten soul is now my meat and I cannot resist chewing on you, just as you cannot resist me. We deserve each other!" The demon came close and took a bite out of Martin's cheek. As he bit, Martin could smell the stench of the substance that the demon was eating, his own soul.

Even as Martin wanted to deny what the demon spoke to him, he could not. For it was true, all true and he knew it. "How I wish I could have found the truth!" He suddenly cried out.

Paul and David had left the gathering as soon as all the people were fed. Janna and Susan were busily ministering to the people, answering questions and gathering leftovers from the meal. As Paul and David travelled toward the hospital, they gave glory to God for the fantastic day and the abundant provision of food that had been given to them. As they gave God the glory, a praise song began to ascend from their lips to the heavens and the presence of the Holy Spirit grew stronger upon them.

Taralah and Putiel, Paul and David's guardian angels, flew alongside. They too were caught up on the glorious praise song to the Father. They could feel the power come from above as the Holy Spirit gave them strength. Whenever the saints join in thanksgiving and praise, the angels begin to vibrate with the presence of the One who is all majesty and power.

"Tonight we will fight with the stronghold demon known as Dimnah. His name means 'Dung-heap' because he is the one who carries off the souls who have just died without receiving mercy. He takes them and begins to feed off of them, and especially seems to like the bowels." Taralah spoke with disgust. "He has already begun to devour the man Martin, even before the man has died. This demon thinks there will be no fight for this man. These two have prayed though, and we shall fight this demon and take his supper from him!" Taralah drew out his sword and swung it through the air in anticipation. The sword glistened with fire, flashing as it flew back and forth.

Putiel laughed and drew his sword also. "I love to fight for even the least of the humans. It will be wonderful to tear this demon apart from the man. If more followers could believe that God will save even the most sinful men, even on their deathbed if only the prayer of faith is prayed, then we could stay busy with the fight. Wouldn't it be wonderful?" Putiel glanced at Taralah.

Taralah had grown serious with the conversation. He sighed and looked longingly at Paul and David. "It is very close to that even now. These two men will bring many into a new faith. Once again faith will be realized on this part of the earth among earthen vessels. We will be very busy from now until the last minute, Putiel. Also know this, the enemy will know that his hour is short. He will bring a deeper darkness and horrible things upon the land. Those who follow him will persecute these men even to death, as it was in the days of the first 12 disciples. A great war is ahead for us all. We must be prepared to fight, for it is now until the end." Taralah smiled at Putiel, "It will be wonderful though, even with the darkness. I have seen what great darkness does to the saints who have all their hope in the Savior. It causes them to grow strong and full of grace more than any other time. It almost seems as if oppression is a blessed gift the way it causes them to rely on the Master."

Paul and David were pulling into the parking lot of the hospital. The two men got out of the car and began to walk toward the entrance. The angels walked very close to the men, swords drawn and ready. Behind them a great host of fighting angels was also on the alert and ready for the war to rage between light and darkness.

Paul turned toward David, "I feel as if we are going in to battle for this man's life, David. Let's stop here and pray quickly before we enter the building, okay?" Paul turned off to the side and stood against the concrete wall of the parking garage. It was empty except for the two of them.

David stopped alongside Paul. "Yes, I agree. Shall I pray?" Paul nodded yes. "Lord, we come to You again and intercede for the life of this man, Martin. We believe that You have given Your life so that all could be saved and that Your desire is that not one would perish. Whatever condition that he is in, Lord, we know that You hold the keys of life and death in Your hands and we call out on behalf of this man in agreement that he should not perish without one more opportunity to know You. Bring him back from the coma that he is in and fill us with Your Holy Spirit so that we can share the truth of the gospel with him. In Jesus Name, we agree that it is done. Amen."

Both Paul and David felt the welling up of the Spirit in their midst. They looked at each other and smiled, as did the two angels that accompanied them. Paul spoke, "This should be good!" He smiled. David nodded as they headed up the stairs toward the hospital entrance.

Chapter Thirty-Five

Martin felt as if an eternity had passed in that horrible place. The demon continued to mock him, and call him stupid. He chewed and chewed upon him. The pain was horrible, the darkness worse. He wondered how he would be able to endure the torture forever. Then he realized that there was no choice. It was not like on the earth. He had been able to escape his momentary pain by drinking and carousing with women. Here it was eternally in his face. There was no place to run. He thought of the lies that he had been told, and that he had told about there being no hell. He had believed that he was responsible for his own mistakes and there was only himself to reckon with. He thought that if he killed himself, he would simply cease to exist. It would be like going into some dreamless sleep, like every night on the earth. He had loved to sleep, and thought that death would be similar. Oh how blind he had been.

He thought of that David fellow who had tried to help him. *If only I had listened to him. I might have been able to find out about what that demon was talking about. Surely that man would not be subject to a place like this. He was too clean. He had such a light and a hope about him. He was different from any man I have ever known. Why didn't I listen?* Martin stopped to cry out again at the pain. The demon was chewing on his face again, and even seemed to slow down and relish eating on his tongue. *Was there no sacred place with this thing?* Martin thought as he wished he could pull his tongue away from the foul creature. The demon hissed at Martin and spoke like a snake. "I love the tongue because you used it for the purpose of deception. It is more foul than any part of the body because of its power."

David and Paul had arrived at the Nurses Station outside the room where Martin's body lie. The Nurse was patiently trying to explain that the man was basically dead already even though his organs had not ceased to function yet. "It won't be long. Are you some sort of clergy? I think it is too late for that sort of thing." She looked at them impatiently.

"We just want to see him. Would that be okay Miss?" Paul spoke with an authority that caused the Nurse to back away. "Suit yourself. He's in room 17. Right over there." She pointed as she walked off down the sterile hallway to answer a call light that had been ringing repeatedly.

As they walked into the room, they could both sense the darkness that seemed to hover over Martin's body. Without speaking, they seemed to know what to do. David walked over to one side of the bed and Paul to the other. They joined hands over the man, and began to pray out loud.

"In the name of Jesus Christ, Satan release this man. We claim him for the kingdom of God." Paul spoke with an authority that he knew was not his own as David agreed.

Martin felt the demon jerk himself free from his meal and cry out. "Hey! What's going on here?" Then demon seemed to have left for the moment and Martin relished in the momentary relief of pain. The demon was screaming in a loud voice. "You can't come in here! He is mine. He doesn't have the blood. You can't have him." The demon seemed to be pulling at Martin, as if holding on in a tug of war. Suddenly a bright light arched across the room, with flashes of light bouncing around in the darkness. Martin felt the presence of power as the two angels began to make war with the demon. Putiel and Taralah were at their best as the demon cowered in fear and tried to fight back. It was useless as the two angels were fully empowered through the faith of the praying men. They loved this type of battle, where they were not held back by unbelief and doubt. As the swords swung through the air, and the demon was cut apart, the light of God illuminated the darkness and brought peace to the poor soul who had suffered under the evil menace.

Martin felt himself being brought out of the darkness. He moved his fingers, then his toes. Slowly he began to open his eyes. As his eyes focused, he could not help but smile. David was there. It was not too late. A second chance.

Martin slowly sat up in the bed. Paul and David smiled and waited. Martin began to speak, slowly stammering at first, but with deep urgency. "Tell me how to find God! I must know the way now. I have been to hell and I know that it is real. I want to know the truth. I'm ready. Tell me please!" He had grabbed hold of David's hand and he was looking at him imploringly.

"Yes, Martin, I will tell you about the way. You will be safe now. God loves you and he has given you His only Son. Jesus Christ went into the regions of the damned and He overcame death for all who would call upon His name. Call upon the name of Jesus, Martin, and you will be saved!" David lovingly embraced the man.

Martin began to weep. "Jesus, please save me. I know that I deserve to be in hell forever. I am the worst sinner ever, I killed my own daughter, and I don't deserve Your mercy. I didn't mean to do it, she was just a little baby and she tried to follow me. But I had been drinking and I was not watching when I backed the car out of the garage. Can You ever forgive me for this horrible sin? Can you save me Lord?

Have mercy on me!" Martin broke down and sobbed even louder. The tears that flowed had been bottled up for years, bottled up in strong drink, and in deep denial. Now they came forth, sorrow, true repentance, need for salvation, it all came forth as Martin opened the door of his heart for the first time in his life.

Paul spoke. "Martin, listen to me. Your daughter is safe with Jesus. Little ones are safe with Him. She was too little to make her choice, He knows that and she is safe with Him. Listen to me Martin, she is not suffering. One day you will see her again. She is with Him even now." Paul held Martin's hand and looked deeply into his eyes trying to convince him of the truth.

Martin began to calm down as Paul spoke. "I believe you. Thank you for telling me this. I want to serve this Savior Jesus from now on. He will be my life. Thank you for saving me Lord!" Again Martin began to cry, this time with tears of joy. Over and over he cried out to God, thanking Him for the rescue from hell, for taking his little girl, for all that He had done to save this wayward soul.

Out in the hallway, the Nurse was wondering at the noise coming from room 17. As she walked firmly across the hallway, she muttered under her breath at the inconsiderate folks that had to come in and upset her routine. She opened the door. "What is going on in here?" She demanded. As she looked up, she saw Martin sitting there smiling at her. She rushed to his side. "This can't be. How can this be? I saw the EEG. You are brain dead. You had a flat line for brain activity. I don't understand." The Nurse walked over to the side of the room and sat in a chair, her face pale from the shock of seeing this dead man raised.

Martin spoke. "I was dead. I was in hell and let me tell you that it is very real. I didn't believe in hell and I found out that it doesn't matter what I believe, there really is a hell. These men prayed for me, and I was given a second chance.

Do you believe in Jesus?" Martin began to declare of his salvation to the Nurse.

Paul and David smiled at each other. Taralah and Putiel also smiled. The host of angels around them began to sing the wonderful songs of heaven that is their privilege whenever a soul is saved.

Later on, as David and Paul drove back toward the park, they once again began to praise God for the wonderful gift of His Son, Jesus Christ. "Wonderful things are going to come of Martin. I believe that he was literally snatched from the mouth of the enemy. He will do great wonders for the kingdom of God." Paul began to prophesy about Martin.

When they arrived at the park, Susan, Janna and the girls were having quite a discussion with several of the women of the park. They were sitting in a tight circle, each so engrossed in the conversation that they did not see the guys as they returned.

David nudged Paul and pointed. "Who is that girl? Did she come with you and Janna?" He was looking at Susan.

"Oh, I'm sorry David. Didn't I introduce you? Susan is staying with us. She has quite a story to tell herself. Why don't you come over to the house tonight and I will introduce you two properly?"

"I would like that Paul. I feel free to go now. I would like to know more about her. She has a light about her that is very special." David could not help staring at Susan.

Chapter Thirty-Six

Later that night as they sat around the dining table at Paul and Janna's house, Susan and David were finally introduced. The talk was excited among all of them, there had been so many wonderful things that had happened. Also, there was a strong desire with each of them to know the other more fully. Finally, as the clamor died down a bit, Paul spoke.

"David, please tell us about yourself. How did you come here? Are you from this area? Do you live in the park, or do you live somewhere else and minister there only?" Paul inquired with interest. He sat forward in his chair, arms resting on the table, hands grasping his coffee cup.

David took a deep breath and slowly let it out. "I was afraid that you would want to know. I do not believe in holding anything back, and if after hearing my story, if you are not comfortable being around me, then I will leave."

"Nonsense David. There is nothing that you could have done that would make us feel that way about you. Please feel free to share your heart with us. We are all sinners covered by the blood of Jesus!" Paul took David's hand and warmly embraced it as he spoke.

"Okay, here goes." David looked up at each one, and when his eyes met Susan's eyes he could not help but let them linger for a moment.

Susan felt her cheeks turn hot and red as David looked at her. She also had been watching the man with interest, for what reason though, she knew not. David was tall, blond headed and handsome. His skin was tanned and his smile easy, with clear blue eyes that sparkled as he spoke.

"I was just recently released from prison for murder." David spoke bluntly and without emotion. Again he turned and looked at each one in the room. His eyes questioned whether or not he should speak further or just leave.

After a long moment of silence, Paul spoke. "In the Ancient book, Jesus once said that if you hate someone in your heart it is the same as murder." He sighed deeply. "I am the most guilty of murder, before I knew of Jesus love, I hated many men." Paul lifted his eyes toward David. The look of compassion was unmistakable.

David smiled weakly at Paul. Again he turned toward Susan. He needed to know how she felt also. He looked questioningly at her.

Susan gazed into David's eyes. She could not help but remember her recent experience of rejecting Jesus and receiving the just punishment for her sin. Compassion began to well up in her heart and tears began to flow freely down her cheeks. David felt himself choke back his own tears as he saw the unconditional love that seemed to flow from this simple young woman. A part of him that he had not known was deeply wounded began to cry out for acceptance. It seemed as though this woman held the keys of his recovery in her eyes as she intently continued to look at him and into his very heart.

Susan spoke. "I have seen how sin separates all of us from the love of God. David, it does not matter what the content of your sin was. What matters the most is that you have found Jesus and His wonderful saving blood. He brought the atoning sacrifice before the Father and the judgment against all of our sins was nullified." With this comment she swept her hand over each person in the room. "I myself am the worst of all sinners. I saw Jesus and I rejected Him when He had my horrible sins upon His shoulders, yet He did not reject me. He came to me and found me in the worst hell of my own making. He rescued me and brought me out of a horrible pit and set my feet upon a rock. How could I hope any less than this for you?" She held out her hand toward David with the gesture of total freedom and acceptance.

David caught his breath in a deep sob and cried out. "Thank you Jesus! How can I ever thank You enough for saving me? Not only have You saved me, but You have brought me a family of friends." With this he stopped and again looked at each person carefully. "I accept your love and friendship. Thank you!" He stopped as he came again to Susan. Once again he could not help but let his eyes linger over her soft hazel eyes. He took in her gentle beauty and sweet spirit that brought such peace and acceptance to his still mending soul. He could not help but reach out his hand toward her.

Susan saw the need that David had. As he reached out his hand toward her, she felt the Spirit within her encourage her. As their hands touched, it was as if a strong current of love swept over both of them. They clasped hands together for a long moment and somehow both of them felt that their friendship was sealed in that bond. For David, he thought not only of friendship, but of love.

The next day they met in the park. A crowd had already gathered and many people were wanting to hear more about the wonderful Savior Jesus Christ. They were so hungry for freedom, love, and acceptance. Paul and David stepped aside and began to plan what must be done.

"Why don't we have Janna and Susan take the women and girls and go over there?" Paul pointed at some picnic tables off to their left. "They could begin teaching the women and helping them with their problems. We can take the men here and begin working with them. Then we can meet at lunchtime and share a meal. Janna was able to gather quite a bit of food and bring it and I see that they are already setting up the soup pot to simmer. How does that sound to you David?" Paul spoke excitedly.

"I think that is an excellent idea. Do you think Susan and Janna will be okay with that? These women here are so in need of guidance and direction in their lives. It would be good to see them receive some of Janna's motherly love." David pondered the idea.

"Why don't we just ask them?" Paul left to get Janna and Susan.

As he was walking away, David stood and watched Susan from a distance, he could not help but be smitten by her. And yet he cautioned himself that to expect her love in return would be a miracle indeed. As he was lost in thought, he did not hear the man who was approaching him.

Martin tapped David gently on the shoulder. David turned around and gasped in surprise. He almost did not recognize Martin. So changed in appearance he was that David had to ask to make sure.

"Martin? Is that you?" David inquired.

"Yes, it's me alright. Ha ha, I bet you didn't expect to see me so soon. When you pray, watch out. God has so totally healed me that they discharged me from the hospital. The doctors were at a total loss as to why I am still alive, and why I am so healthy. I think I embarrassed them. They like to understand everything that happens and I really stumped them." Martin bent over toward David's ear and laughed. "Actually, its kind of fun to see the looks of unbelief on their faces." His eyes danced with a light and joy that made David laugh out loud.

"I am so glad that you are here. God has truly done wonders in you Martin. You must share what God has done for you with all the others." David put his arm around Martin's shoulder and began walking with him over to the group of gathering men. Paul was getting everything set up for them.

"I will be glad to share what God has done for me, but more than that, I want to learn everything I can about God. I want to be taught about the Ancient book and how to follow Jesus. Will you teach me David?" Martin took hold of David's hand imploringly.

"Yes Martin that's what we are about to begin doing here." David led him to a bench and they sat down.

David asked Paul to go first and he sat alongside of Martin while Paul shared.

"Love is patient and kind. Love does not strive for its own way, but it stands back and desires the best for others. Our God is Love, pure love, and in Him is no darkness. To follow after Him is to follow after Love. Love will lay down its life for those around him. If you want to know God, then follow after this love and you will not miss Him. It is this Love that motivated Him to give His only Son for you. He gave Him up for the sake of seeing you all saved from hell. To be a follower of this kind of Love, is to also be willing to lay down your life for others. To see them saved even if it means that you would die for them. Love is the motivation and it is the truth of the gospel that you will find by studying the Ancient book."

Paul stopped for a moment and looked over the crowd of men. "If you want to follow Jesus, then you must lay down your own life and pick up His life. When you were baptized it meant that when you went down into the water, you died to your old sinful nature. And when you came up out of the water, you were reborn into a new creation. You are now sons of the living God. We will not teach you about religion. We will not point you in the direction of certain doctrines or truths. These are things that each man must find for himself as he studies the Ancient book, but we will strive for unity among all the brethren so long as this unity is based in the atoning blood of Jesus Christ. Our focus here is to point you in the direction of the cross and to teach you how to find the call that He has for you individually. Each one of you has a calling and a place in the body of which we are all a part. If we can show you how to find that place, and teach, and shepherd you into that truth then we will have accomplished our goal. We are not here to make clones of ourselves, but to help you find who you are in Him. Do not look to us or our ministry among you as the answer, or we will have done you harm. Find Jesus Christ as we point Him out to you, and find Him for yourselves. We cannot save you, only He can. Each one of you must find Him and know Him for your-selves. The Ancient book teaches us that Christ is head over the man. If you want to be fulfilled in all that you are called to be, then do not look to man as your head, but to Christ. Each one of you is important to His kingdom. Each one of you is to be trained up to go out and serve Him. There are many who are lost around us, and I commission you now to tell them and bring them to Jesus. You may feel ignorant about some things and that is okay. Be willing to admit that you don't know everything. The only thing that matters the most is that Jesus is the only way of salvation. There is no other way. Ask the Holy Spirit to guide you and give you answers to their questions. He is freely given to you."

"David and I will be here to help you and encourage you in your journey. But you must remember not to place us above Jesus. We are merely His servants. Men like you. He is the only One you can rely on. He will always be with you, He will never forsake you. We are fallible and He is not.

David will begin teaching you from the Ancient book. Tomorrow we will bring more copies of the Ancient book to pass out. If you cannot read let us know. My wife is going to be having a reading class at our house, we will bus you there and teach you how to read. If you have any needs or questions don't be afraid to ask. We will use whatever resources available to help you. God is going to supply our needs. He is going to open the doors for us to share this wonderful news of the gospel with many." Paul stopped and smiled. He felt such an encouragement of love coming from the Holy Spirit.

David stood and joined Paul. "I think that we should pray now. Lets give thanks to God for the wonderful salvation that He has brought to so many of you in the last few days."

As David began to pray, Paul wondered at how God would begin to move among these people, and how the enemy would try to stop them.

Chapter Thirty-Seven

Several months passed and the little fellowship of people grew daily. Different people heard of the powerful moving of the Spirit, including people of influence and wealth. Several large warehouse buildings were supplied and housing was made available. Teaching and counselling was offered daily, many of the local Churches were invited to join and be a part of the fellowship. Few responded to the offer however, homeless people not being a prize for a parishioner. Some Churches did respond and Paul and David were able to point the people in the direction of Church fellowship that would help them to continue to grow.

David and Susan became closer and closer, finding that common bond in the Spirit, and a deep attraction toward one another. Susan loved David more than she ever thought was possible, his gentle manner, laughing eyes, and depth of compassion for others was very appealing to her. He was ten years older than Susan, but it really didn't matter, they fit together and the ministry they both desired was a common interest that sealed their love. David was slow at showing Susan his love, wondering if it was really possible that he could find love again after his horrible past and all that he had been through, and yet he hoped continually. Susan was everything he ever wanted in a mate and more. She loved God with such a passion and depth, a light always came forth in her eyes that showed her connections to the kingdom of Heaven. That she loved him back was almost more than he could bear, God was so good to him. Finally, after all the hints had been made, David got the courage to ask Susan to be his wife. He would never forget the moment.

They had just finished feeding the poor, and were both washing dishes in the clean up effort. She had teasingly tossed some suds onto his face, a gentle smile playing at the corners of her mouth. He stopped and stared at her, not really responding to her playfulness. She stepped back in wonder at the look that he was giving her, not quite understanding what he was up to. Then he just blurted it out ... "Susan, I love you more than words can tell, please marry me and make me the happiest man in the world."

She was amazed, and yet the sincerity of his proclamation was doubtless. She looked into those deep blue eyes and waited, listening for the Spirit within her to respond first. Wanting to jump and scream out her love back to him, and yet holding on to her emotions. She waited. David began to wonder and Susan saw his eyes begin to cloud with doubt. Then the Spirit came and encouraged her, deep in her heart she knew this was God's plan for her life.

"David, I love you very deeply. You have become my best friend and confidant. I could not imagine being separated from you ever, yes my love, I will marry you!" Her hazel eyes glistened with tears and her smile deepened as he came forward to seal the promise with a long awaited kiss.

Meanwhile, the whole earth was experiencing great birth pangs of the soon coming end of all things as they are known. Persecution against the Remnant was increasing, first in communistic, iron rule countries, second and slowly in so-called free countries. Those who had hardened themselves against the light of the gospel were filled with the same demonic hatred as the devil himself, for his time was short and he planned to exit the history of the planet earth with as many of the human creation as he could deceive.

In the heavens, excitement and anticipation filled the air as the angels met once again to discuss the battle plan for the coming days. The angels gathered at the big round table as the meeting that had been called by Michael the Archangel began.

"The time has come for the signs and wonders to be released again in the earth. Up until now, there have only been pockets of power, but now it is time for the outpouring of the latter rain. The enemy is very angry because he knows that his time is short. Crime and violence are increasing at unprecedented rates. A spirit of cruelty and murder is loose in the land and many people are so full of fear that their hearts are failing them. The religious order of the day has not brought them answers, neither has the government. The Remnant has been prepared with the grace and humility of our Lord Jesus and they will move in power and anointing."

"The cross has been shown to them and they know the power of it. They have embraced the cross and not conformed to the ways of the flesh. They have buffeted their bodies and given their flesh over to be chastised so that the Spirit is in charge." The great angel stopped and looked over each of the angels. He could not help but smile as he thought of how close they were to the fulfillment of all things.

"The Lamb of God has prepared the great feast and yet there are still many to be invited to the marriage supper of the Lamb. The time of the gentiles is coming to a close. It is time for the last great outpouring upon the earth. It is time to bring the Remnant into the greater works that the Master spoke of.

They are ready." Again the angel paused, he became very sober in his appearance.

"I must warn you. This is a time of great victory and great passion. The enemy has felt the hour of his confinement approaching and he is angry. He has stretched forth his arm in every direction of the world and spoken this command to the entire demonic horde: 'Wreak havoc.' He knows that his greatest stronghold is among those who call themselves Christians and are not. Those who follow this Antichrist spirit are full of his power, and even the elect would be deceived if that were possible. It would be possible if it were not for the great amount of grace that the Holy Spirit is pouring out on those who have humbled themselves and sought the cross over the luxuries of the flesh. You have been called to minister and protect, to encourage and serve them, the elect. You must stay close and follow the leading of the Spirit. Some will be put to death and others will be removed from dangerous situations, according to the Father's will. Be alert and ready at all times to follow His commands." Michael stood then and as he did his appearance began to shine brighter and brighter. Soon the entire room was so full of majesty that many of the angels began to sing out praises to the Father. Michael acknowledged that he was finished with his discourse and the angels broke forth in even more wondrous praises as the heavens vibrated with glory and worship.

Adaiah thought of how the brilliance of Michael was so like that of Lucifer, before the fall. Lucifer was so beautiful that many of the angels had bowed before him and Lucifer had taken the glory and become so proud that he was no longer able to stay within the realm of heaven. God will not share His glory with another. As he looked at Michael and saw the pure humility on the angels' face, he was glad that Michael did not follow in Lucifer's footsteps. He was so different from that other angel. He loved the Master and followed Him so closely, he was a true servant.

Chapter Thirty-Eight

D avid came running breathlessly into the office. "Paul, quick, call a meeting as soon as you can, get everyone together, we must warn them and our time is short!"

"Whoa, hold on man! What are you talking about?" Paul stood up from his desk and walked over toward David.

"It's happening now, Paul. They are going to start arresting us for our participation in what they call a rebellion against authority. We must leave now, as soon as possible. The Alliance of Religious Order has joined forces against us, they have declared law against those who refuse to follow the system they have set in place. They say we have discriminated against them by refusing to have their teachers on our staff. I tried to tell them that we don't have a staff, that we are just a simple gathering of people in Jesus Name, but that just angered them all the more. They have new laws passed and they're gaining power since they are made up of so many political and gay rights activists. It's like they have taken in all the different activists and joined up together against the true church. In fact they are calling themselves: 'The Universal Truth.' The government has finally sanctioned them with control over the church so that the political energies of the country can focus solely upon the economy without having to spend time deciphering what is political and what interferes with separation of church and state. They have been given the same clout as the United Nations since they are universally based. They have their own military segment that is sponsored by the tax payer now, and they can arrest any whom they believe are interfering in their goal."

David sat down hard in a chair, out of breath. Paul just stood and stared at him. "I can't believe that it has come to this. David, do you realize that we are living in times that are spoken of in the book of Revelation? John saw these things come to pass in a vision, and now we are experiencing them."

They continued to stare at each other in silence. Finally after a few moments Paul cleared his throat. "I think it is time for the underground church to be born in America. We must call a meeting tonight, from now on we will have to meet in small, inconspicuous groups. We must increase our witnessing and lead as many to the Lord as possible. I believe that God is going to open the flood gates of heaven and there will be a great ingathering of souls. I heard that in Israel many of the Jews have realized Jesus Christ as their Messiah and there is a great celebration going on over there. The time is so short, David!"

"Yes, you are right. We must begin our plan for the underground church. We must prepare for persecution! We have taught that death could be the cost of our faith one day, and now I can see that it is on the doorstep. Every since the change to universal money last month I have been feeling that things are speeding up. Now that everyone is required to use a card for most financial transactions, it won't be long until we must take a mark of some type, probably a computer chip in our hand, to hold all our financial records. I have seen many people who have refused to use the card.

The black market and bartering are in full swing in the underground already. The banks have declared that the end of this year they will quit issuing paper money and by the end of next year they will no longer accept any paper money at all, it will be useless." David paused and smiled.

"I have asked the Lord whether or not we should try and stock up on food and things, but He has reassured me that He will supply our needs even as He did Elijah during the time of drought. It is so exciting to live in these days!" David gleamed with anticipation.

Paul patted David on the back and laughed. "You seem excited at the thought of persecution. You surely are a strange creature!"

"How can I help it? Do you realize how close we are to the beginning of our true life, of heaven and seeing Him face to face? What greater joy than to know that the hour is near, even at the threshold." David whooped and jumped for joy. "I always knew I would be one of the martyr's."

"Speaking of being a martyr, what about the wedding? Are you and Susan still planning on being married day after tomorrow?" Paul inquired jokingly.

"You bet we are! Then we are going to hit the streets. We have a route all planned out of how we are going to spread the gospel over the prison systems up north. We have that old camper that you restored for our honeymoon cottage and we are set for ministry. We can't wait, only now it will be more interesting with having to dodge the Universalist's." David replied. "Now let's call the meeting and get this place shut down!"

"Sounds like a plan to me." Paul agreed.

Taralah and Putiel were there, swords drawn in anticipation of the coming days. The world seemed as though it were rocking back and forth on the edge of a great precipice. Anger and rage had infiltrated the planet, causing murder and lawlessness in unprecedented numbers. Little children were murderers. Grown men were amazed at the cruelty that the lawless children could muster. Evil was rampant, and yet the Light of God was being poured out increasingly. Where the Light was allowed to penetrate, there were whole cities aflame for God, and where the darkness was allowed to rule, there was every kind of evil gone mad. Cities seemed to be divided according to whether the darkness ruled or the Light ruled. There were no more gray areas as there had been in the 80's and 90's. Watching the Saints in their determination was wonderful for the angels. Whereas before, many were torn between the lust of worldly things, and serving God, now there was total dedication to the ways of God. Sharing provision and taking care of one another had returned as it had once been in the early church. The saints declared, "Yes, I am my brother's keeper."

Adaiah appeared just then as the angels were talking. He glowed even more than he had before, so much had changed. "I watch these Christians and I am so amazed at their strength of calling and desire to follow the Lord. I remember when all this was a plan, and now here we are, with mature followers who will give up everything to follow the Savior." He smiled at the remembrance of all the years with his charge, Bilshan, waiting for the time of her salvation. Now there were countless lives saved and brought into the kingdom on account of this small company of believers. Revival had broken out at Riverside Park and continued there to this day. Martin was a leader of the move as many came to him for healing from alcohol and abuse. Tent cities had been erected due to the salvation of the Mayor of that city, and over half of the city itself had come to salvation. Bars had closed, churches had renewal, there were no longer hungry lost people wondering about without homes. It was amazing to the angel how much could happen when just a few believers decide to stand on the truth without wavering.

The angels separated at this point, each following his charge, light and joy emanating from them and filling the atmosphere.

The day wore on and soon the building was full of people. David and Paul stood up at the front. David was the first to speak. He stood on a makeshift stage and looked all around the room. Recognizing faces here and there, SaraJean there in front with her husband John, Janna and the girls next to them, countless others who had been faithful to the move of God. He smiled and laughed out loud.

"It is so good to see all of you. I'm still amazed at how God could take a man like me, a murderer who deserved death, and bring me here, then give me a family of this proportion. It is enough to make a fella cry!" He raised his hands over his head and gave a whoop. At this point the whole room erupted in a cheer for the Lord Jesus Christ. The people clapped and clapped their hands, crying out to their Messiah with thanksgiving. Then the people quieted.

David stood again and began his address. "As you all know, we are living in the final moments of time. There is revival in the earth that has brought millions of people to the saving knowledge of Jesus Christ. We are a part of the end of days, and yet as He promised He saved the best for last." Again the people began to chant their love to the Savior. The room filled with light and several of the angels appeared next to David and Paul. The people were not fazed by their appearance though as these things had become more and more common in their meetings. The angels joined in the praise of the Father of Creation. The room became glittery with gold dust that infiltrated the atmosphere, and the people raised the level of their worship even more. David realized that the people needed to worship God at this time and sat back down. A band began to play songs of worship and people began to dance and worship with all their might. After several hours of worship a lull came over the room and the people sat down in anticipation of what was next. Paul sensed that it was time for him to speak and he came forward.

"It is time for this phase of our operation to end. We will be closing the doors of the warehouse buildings in the next week. It is time for the underground church to begin. You have been trained up in the faith. You are all leaders in this movement, it is time to go out and find the final lost ones who are yet to inherit the kingdom. Make your homes a sanctuary, invite your neighbors, your co-workers, it is time to finalize our lives here. You have been taught that persecution is possible. Now the laws have been passed making it illegal to follow Jesus Christ in freedom. If you are so inclined by the Spirit, continue your ministry. If you are arrested, there is a possibility that you will be eventually put to death for your beliefs." At this the people jumped up from their seats, at least a thousand people were in that meeting, and shouted with all their might... "Yes, and amen. We will serve our Lord, even to the death, for we are heirs of the Eternal Kingdom of God." Once again the excitement and worship hit a crescendo, people were dancing in great joy and victory. Paul could hear little children proclaiming their places on the martyr thrones, as they danced in circles and whooped with great joy. He too joined in the clamor.

The angels danced with all their might at the great celebration of these people who were so caught up with the prospect of eternal life that they would gladly give up their temporal lives. More and more angels appeared and joined in the dancing until it seemed that all the people would be caught up into the heavens even now.

After another hour of intense worship the room quieted again. This time David stood up and spoke again. "It has been such a pleasure to work alongside each of you. There is such a diversity of gifts here. You are all so special to me." He stopped and looked carefully around the room. Clearing his voice, he continued. "Remember to encourage one another. Whatever comes our way in the next months and years, always remember this, do not forsake meeting together whenever you can. Pray for one another, encourage one another in the ministry. We all need each other, and together we make up the whole body of Christ. If the enemy cuts us down, come together even stronger than before. Take care of each others families if some are taken and others left. We know that in the fulness of time our Lord is going to come on a white horse and we will ride with Him in victory. Our victory in not found in the flesh, it is found in Him, no matter what happens. Keep your focus on the eternal kingdom not on that which is perishing. Stay strong to the end if you are called on to give your life for Him. He will be there with you and help you. I know this as a fact. He came to me in a vision and showed me that the suffering unto death was special to Him. He would be with any who would take the step of faith and follow Him to the cross. Trust God with all your heart, He will never leave you or forsake you."

"If they take the Ancient book away from you, remember that your faith is found in the Kingdom of God, not in paper. The kingdom is within you. That can never be taken away. Stand firm in your faith and do not waver. Listen to the Holy Spirit for He lives inside you and will speak to you if you will listen. He is not set apart for the privileged, but He is available for any who receive Him. If your enemy strikes you on the cheek, turn the other cheek and do not become bitter. Forgive your enemy even as God has forgiven you. The Spirit will enable you to do this. All you need to do is ask. Remember that God has waiting for you an eternal life that is beyond your wildest dreams. His love and enduring power will give you what you need to lay down your life for him. We are called to be the last, and the entire body of Christ that has gone on before us is watching. Let us be strong in the faith and go forth in great victory, bringing honor and glory to our Savior as the final chapter of life on this planet comes to a close. We are more than conquerors in Christ Jesus and we want to prove ourselves as the best wine that came last!"

Once again the people erupted in great cheers. Paul called out that the meeting was over, and there would be all night prayer and worship as the people felt led. He then joined with the other worshippers who found great joy in hoping that they would be able to stand in the time of great darkness that preceded the end.

Epilogue

David and Susan planned to be married in a simple ceremony, then travel about sharing the gospel wherever the Spirit would lead them. As their friends came forward to wish them well, many sensed that this could be their last gathering here on the earth. Paul and Janna were excited, and yet quiet at the thought of separating. David and Susan would be traveling, ministering in different cities as they felt led, and Paul and Janna would be staying put, encouraging the local body in the faith. Miracles of great healing had begun to take place in the meetings, and people were pouring in from all over to find help in their hour of need. Horrible diseases had come upon the human race for which there was no cure outside the miraculous, and God had begun to move in these ways. People were raised from the dead, healed of horrible disease, and set free from more horrid sin. The Universalists were angry at the move of God, and more laws were being passed to try and prevent the so-called extremists from continuing their practices. Gay rights and other perverse moves were confident in their stand, fighting against the God who said what they did was sin. The Remnant was pressing into the depths of Jesus Christ and following the Spirit. The gospel would be preached in every corner of the earth, and time was coming to a close.

As David and Susan bid their friends goodbye, Paul and Janna joined them in a prayer.

"Father. We are so thankful to You for all that You have done. How could we ever begin to thank you for all Your gifts to us, especially the wonderful gift of Your son, Jesus Christ?

As we separate ways, we ask that You would go before us, that the Holy Spirit would guide us into all truth, and that You would use us to fully bring the gospel of salvation and hope to this earth. We love each other so much and thank You for giving us each other. Bless us with Your great grace, empower us with Your Presence that we could be and do all that You have created for us to be and do.

We long for the final day, when You return and reign once again over that which You have created. We long for the day when we will be together again, not only in body, but in the perfection that You have planned for us on the resurrection day. And we long for the day when Satan will be chained and stopped from his evil. The day when You will wipe away every tear, and bring the wonderful gathering of the saints. We long for You Father, for Your Son, and for the Holy Spirit and our eternal life to begin."

The End